CELTIC GODS AND HEROES

Marie-Louise Sjoestedt

DOVER PUBLICATIONS, INC.
Mineola, New York

Bibliographical Note

This Dover edition, first published in 2000, is an unabridged reprint of *Gods and Heroes of the Celts,* originally published by Methuen & Co. Ltd., London, 1949. Translated from the French *Dieux et heros des Celtes,* and with a preface, by Myles Dillon.

Library of Congress Cataloging-in-Publication Data

Sjoestedt, Marie-Louise, 1900–1940.
   [Dieux et héros des Celtes. English]
   Celtic gods and heroes / Marie-Louise Sjoestedt.
       p. cm.
   Originally published: Gods and heroes of the Celts. London : Methuen, 1949.
   Includes bibliographical references and indexes.
   ISBN 0-486-41441-8 (pbk.)
   1. Gods, Celtic. 2. Heroes—Mythology—Ireland. 3. Mythology, Celtic. 4. Celts—Religion. I. Title.

BL900 .S48313 2000
299'.16—dc21

00-034637

Manufactured in the United States of America
Dover Publications, Inc., 31 East 2nd Street, Mineola, N.Y. 11501

PREFACE

THIS is the last work of the brilliant French scholar whose name it bears. Marie-Louise Sjoestedt was primarily a linguist, and some of her work in Early and Modern Irish is of the first importance. With this book she entered the neglected field of Celtic mythology. *Dieux et Héros des Celtes* was published in Paris in 1940 and has not, I think, been widely noticed. But it deserves the attention of those who are interested in the matter, and I hope that an English translation will bring it to a wide circle of readers.

The author's approach to the problems she discusses is new, and it will probably arouse criticism. She establishes two 'oppositions': for the gods a category of mother-goddesses who are local, rural spirits of fertility or of war, sometimes in animal form, often in triple form, and a category of chieftain-gods who are national, protectors of the people, magicians, nurturers. The marriage of the chieftain-god with the mother-goddess assures the people of protection, and symbolizes the union of man with the fertile soil. For the hero the opposition is between the tribal hero, represented by Cú Chulainn, and the hero outside the tribe, represented by Fionn. The episode in which women are sent to meet Cú Chulainn in his frenzy is represented as the survival of an ancient initiation rite; but Thurneysen would perhaps have regarded it as a genuine chastity-motif (*Heldensage*, 81, 139).

The Book of Conquests, which is here used as a source, is a mediaeval work of fiction (O'Rahilly, *Early Irish History*, 193, 264), so that, while it is the most convenient place of reference for the matter it contains, it remains a secondary witness. With regard to the author's statement that the texts are silent about matters of eschatology (p. xix), it may be said that the Voyages and Vision Tales might have been given more consideration.

But it was not the author's intention, within the scope of this short exposition, to exhaust the subject. Her purpose was to discover what is characteristic of Celtic mythology, and in this direction she has made important progress.

The gods of the Celts, as they are presented here, are quite unlike the gods of classical mythology. They are not patrons of love or war or of various crafts, nor have they a home in heaven. They differ among themselves, within the two categories already mentioned, not so much in function as in name, and it is suggested that the multiple names reflect various local origins. The Irish Other World is not given much prominence, for gods and men dwell together upon Irish soil in an uneasy partnership.

Professor O'Rahilly's *Early Irish History and Mythology* (Dublin, 1946) appeared some years after this book was first published, so that there is no reference to his work. On the other hand, the book was not available to him when he wrote, and he has not pronounced judgment upon it. At some points there is conflict of opinion, for O'Rahilly regards Cú Chulainn and Fionn as originally identical, whereas here they are presented as opposite types. But the scope and method of the two books is so different that there is not much ground for disagreement, and beside the massive learning and detailed evidence of O'Rahilly's study, readers will welcome this summary account. Within its small compass the author has used to great advantage her splendid gifts of interpretation and synthesis, together with balanced judgment and wide perspective.

The work of translation has been an act of piety to the memory of a friend whose death is a grave loss to Celtic studies. Some additional notes have been supplied by the translator, and a few items have been added to the bibliography for the benefit of English readers. The early recension of the *Book of Conquests* has been substituted for O'Clery's version in the quotation on p. 5, as Macalister's edition of the former was not available to the author.

M.D.

CONTENTS

ABBREVIATIONS

CIL *Corpus Inscriptionum Latinarum*

LU R.I. BEST AND OSBORN BERGIN, *Lebor na Huidre* (Dublin, 1929)

RC *Revue Celtique*

SPAW *Sitzungsberichte der preussischen Akademie der Wissenschaften*

Thurneysen, *Heldensage* R. Thurneysen, *Die irische Helden- und Königsage* (Halle, 1921)

ZCP *Zeitschrift für Celtische Philologie*

INTRODUCTION

THIS little book does not attempt to give a general account, however summary, of the Celtic mythologies. There are good studies in which the known facts have been collected, and it would have been superfluous to repeat them. These works are cited in the bibliography. I have abstained, too, from attempting a comparative interpretation of the myths, not because the attempt would be vain in itself, but because it seemed better to leave comparison to the specialists. If a student of Celtic can put into some order the rather confused traditions, it is by staying upon his own ground. This outline is intended only to present some groups of facts which may be regarded as characteristic of the Celtic attitude towards mythology, and to present them from the point of view of Celtic studies, and even, so far as possible, from the point of view of the Celt himself.

This prescription involves two corollaries. On the one hand, one must free oneself from conceptions borrowed from outside, and particularly from those of Greek or Roman tradition. It would seem that that goes without saying; and yet the religious notions inherited from the classical world have such a hold on the imagination of western man that we have difficulty in not introducing them even where they are out of place. When we are tackling a strange mythology, we seek instinctively an Olympus where the gods abide, an Erebus, kingdom of the dead, a hierarchy of gods, specialized as patrons of war, of the arts or of love. And, seeking them, we do not fail to find them. Caesar is a good example of this error. He does not hesitate to recognize among the Gaulish gods Mars,

Mercury, Apollo, Jupiter and Minerva.[1]   Did the Celts
acknowledge a similar division of functions?   Had they a
notion of their deities comparable to that which the Greeks
and Romans had of theirs?   It is important to consider the
question without prejudice.

On the other hand, if we must ask the Celts themselves
for the key to their mythology, it is proper to believe the
evidence they have left us, unless there is proof to the
contrary. This too would seem to go without saying; and
yet it must be said, if only to avoid the reproach of naïvety.
The mythographers of mediaeval Ireland have drawn a
picture of Celtic paganism so different from what we know,
or think we know, of Indo-European paganism that it at
first arouses suspicion.   When they describe the ancient
gods as prehistoric tribes who once laboured and fought
upon the soil of Ireland, and still dwell there invisibly
present, side by side with the human inhabitants, there is a
great temptation to see in this notion, for which there is an
analogy in various primitive mythologies, the result of a
secondary process of euhemerization, or of a confusion
between the gods and the fairies or the dead. I believe that
we should not dismiss lightly the evidence of the texts.
Those who composed them were indeed Christians, but
only a few generations separated them from paganism. Our
manuscript tradition takes us back in many instances to the
eighth century, when the conversion of Ireland, begun in
the fifth century, was neither very remote nor, probably,
very profound. It is imprudent, therefore, without good
reason, to repudiate the ideas that these authors had of the
mythical world of the Celts, to which they were much
closer than we can ever be. In the belief that there is a
greater risk of error in too much scepticism than in too little,
I have decided to follow the native tradition. It may be
found, in the course of the investigation, that this tradition

---

[1] *De Bello Gallico*, vi, 17, *v. inf.* p. 20.

has remained, down to its latest developments, more faithful to certain constants of primitive imagination than it appears at first.

I have mentioned the mythical world of the Celts. Has this expression any meaning? We do not know the 'Celts', but only Gauls, Irish, Welsh and Bretons. And we know that these peoples differed widely in social organization. Kingship, which plays an important role among the insular Celts, survived only in traces in the Gaul that Caesar knew. On the other hand, our knowledge of the religion of these peoples derives from documents of unequal value, differing in date and in kind. For the Celts of the continent we have the names of deities, figured sculptures of the Gallo-Roman period, some passages of Greek and Latin authors who were always inclined to interpret the fragmentary and summary information they had in the light of their own ideas; for the insular Celts we have an abundant literature, but it is relatively late and marked here and there by Christian influence. Are we justified, under the circumstances, in supposing that there were at least types of religious notions common to the whole area, if not a common mythology? And, if so, can we hope to recover the traces of them from documents that are not exactly comparable?

Of course there can be no question of a Common Celtic period in mythology, such as we suppose for the language. What we know of the decentralized character of society among the Celts, and of the local and anarchical character of their mythology and ritual excludes that hypothesis. There are indeed some striking agreements of detail, as, for example, between the name of the Irish god Lug and that of the *Lugoues* who were worshipped in Spain and Switzerland, or of the city of Lyons, *Lugudunum* ('The Fort of Lug'); between the Badb Catha ('The Raven of Battle'), a warrior-goddess of Ireland, and *Cathubodua* who is mentioned in an inscription of Haute-Savoie; or again between

the champion Ogma and the Gaulish Ogmios described by
Lucan.[1] In the last instance the phonology of the name of
Ogma shows that Irish has here borrowed from Gaulish.[2]
So, too, if we find the Gaulish *Deus Mars Segomo* in Munster,
it is apparently because the cult had been introduced in the
historical period by immigrant communities.[3] One must
therefore be cautious in interpreting as evidence of a
primitive unity correspondences that are sufficiently explained by the close relations, either of peace or of war,
which never ceased to exist among the Celtic peoples
bordering the western seas.

In the absence of common religious origins, we shall seek
certain religious attitudes, certain forms of mythological
imagery that are common to the whole Celtic area. The
names of the deities, and doubtless also the plotting of the
myths, may differ; but the types seem none the less analogous, and, even more than the elements of each system, the
equilibrium which controls them seems here and there to
be similar. The formal contrasts make the structural
resemblance all the more striking.

This structural unity of the Celtic world, as it appears in
the sphere of religion, finds its expression and its explanation
in a social phenomenon, namely the existence in all the
Celtic communities about which we have information of a
class of sacred men, everywhere remarkably similar. It is the
class of druids (Gaulish δρουίδα; Irish *druí*, pl. *druid*; W. *dryw*),
from which that of the poets (Gaulish *bardus*; Irish *bard*;
W. *bardd*; or Gaulish *vātes*; Irish *fáith*) cannot be separated.

This is not the place for a discussion of the druids,[4] nor
for an attempt to define their relationship to the sacred
poets, who seem to have inherited in some Christian Celtic

---

[1] For all the Gaulish names cited, see Holder, *Altkeltischer Sprachschatz s.v.*
[2] Thurneysen, *Beitr. z. Gesch. d. deutschen Spr. u. Lit.* 61, 195, who regards
the Irish and Gaulish names as unrelated [Tr.].
[3] Eoin MacNeill, *Phases of Irish History*, 127.
[4] T. D. Kendrick, *The Druids*.

societies a part of the ancient attributes of the druids. But one cannot understand the conditions in which the myths must have developed, nor their transmission and diffusion, unless one bears in mind the fact that there was a class (not necessarily a caste in the Hindu sense) whose duty it was to preserve the traditions which constitute the religion, the learning and the literature of the social group. The professional organization of this class transcended political divisions (what Caesar tells us of the general druidic assembly, and of the relations between the druids of Gaul and of Britain agrees with what we know of the activities of the official poets of Ireland and Wales), and ensured a certain unity of conception in space, in spite of local differences, while its manner of recruitment and of technical training ensured the permanence of the tradition in time.

The strong cultural tradition of the scholar-magician class of *filid*,[1] the poets of Ireland, and the spiritual continuity which it embodies, are responsible for the survival of traits that are plainly archaic and lead us straight back into pagan times, even in the literature of the later mediaeval period. We shall have occasion to point out that a passage from the epic tales, which in its present form goes back only to the eleventh century, reflects the civilization of La Tène. This archaism, which is characteristic of the continental Celtic world, and even more notably of Ireland, shows itself in unexpected ways, not only in the mythology but also in the ritual. It will be enough to cite one example. I take it from Giraldus Cambrensis, who wrote his *Description of Ireland* about 1185 A.D. In it he describes a 'barbarous and abominable' rite of enthronement practised by an Ulster clan: 'The whole people of that country being gathered in one place, a white mare is led into the midst of them, and he who is to be inaugurated, not as a prince but as a brute, not as a king, but as an outlaw, comes before the people on all fours, con-

---

[1] J. Vendryes, *La Poésie de cour en Irlande et en Galles*, Institut de France, 1932, 18.

fessing himself a beast with no less impudence than imprudence. The mare being immediately killed, and cut in pieces and boiled, a bath is prepared for him from the broth. Sitting in this, he eats of the flesh which is brought to him, the people standing round and partaking of it also. He is also required to drink of the broth in which he is bathed, not drawing it in any vessel, nor even in his hand, but lapping it with his mouth. These unrighteous rites being duly accomplished, his royal authority and dominion are ratified.'[1]

Knowing the attitude of Giraldus to Irish affairs, one might suspect a scandalous calumny, if the authenticity of this ἱερὸς γάμος were not guaranteed by its agreement with another royal rite attested at the opposite side of the Indo-European world, namely the rite which accompanies the horse-sacrifice, the Hindu *asvamedha*.[2] After the wives of the king have made a ceremonial circuit of the victim, the principal spouse (*mahisi*) approaches it and submits to a simulated union which is expounded by the priest in an explicit liturgical commentary. Then the victim is dismembered. While in India it is the king's wife who unites herself to the animal incarnation of the powers of fertility, in Ireland it is the king himself who accomplishes the rite (not symbolically but actually) with a female incarnation of the same powers. This agrees with what we shall see of the part played by the mother-goddesses, who often appear in animal form; and it must be compared with the various mythical episodes describing the union of the chief god with one or other of these deities.

We see that an Irish tribe, though Christianized centuries before, preserved down to the later Middle Ages, and in all its primitive brutality, a hierogamic rite which belongs to the most ancient level of Indo-European religion. It is not an accident that this rite was preserved by the Hindus on the

[1] Giraldus Cambrensis, *Topographia Hibernica*, iii, 25 (tr. Forester).
[2] F. R. Schröder, ZCP 16, 310; C. Clemen, *Religionsgeschichte Europas*, I, 179.

one hand and by the Celts on the other, while the horse-sacrifice, as it appears elsewhere in the Indo-European area, does not present the same sexual character. It is well known that a remarkable similarity of religious vocabulary has been observed in the two fields at opposite extremes of the Indo-European area, and that the similarity can be explained by a feature of social organization, namely the existence in both fields of that class of sacred men to whom we have already referred, the Celtic druids, the Hindu brahmins, and, in a more developed form, the Roman flamens.[1]

This example suffices to prove that late documents may faithfully preserve religious facts which date from very early antiquity. This can often be verified in Ireland, where very archaic forms of art and types of imagery have been kept alive, one may say, down to the present day. We are thus dispensed from offering any excuse for making the Irish tradition the basis of this discussion. It is due not to any personal prejudice but to a necessity inherent in the subject. It is chiefly in Ireland that Celtic paganism survived long enough to be committed to writing. And everything tends to suggest that if the oral tradition of Gaul before the conquest had been written down and had been preserved for us, it would have revealed a mythological world not very different, and certainly not more 'primitive' than that to which the mediaeval Irish texts give access. So, without wishing to attribute to the whole Celtic world the different series of myths which we shall have to consider, I do not think there is any great disadvantage, for the purpose of a general survey such as I propose to outline here, in abstaining from a comparison of the different Celtic peoples one with another, and in using the term 'Celtic' sometimes with reference to facts that are directly attested only in Irish tradition.

[1] Vendryes, *Mém. de la Soc. de Ling.* 20, 265; G. Dumézil, *Flamen-Brahman*, Ann. Musée Guimet, 51.

This Irish tradition is represented by a vast collection of texts.[1] There are prose tales, often interspersed with lyric poems, which modern critics divide into cycles (the Mythological Cycle, the Ulster Cycle, the Ossianic Cycle, the Cycle of the Kings), and which the native scholars classified by types (Raids, Elopements, Voyages, Birth-Tales, Destructions, Death-Tales, etc.). There are didactic and narrative poems like the *Dindshenchas*, a collection of traditions concerning the remarkable places of Ireland; and glossaries and various treatises, such as the glossary of the king-bishop Cormac (†908), or the *Cóir Anmann* ('Etymology of Names'). These are literary documents, of which none is earlier than the eighth century in the form in which we possess it. Hence it is necessary to use them with caution, and one cannot admit an isolated fact as having any religious significance unless it is confirmed by comparison with the other features of ritual or mythology, for it may be a secondary embellishment. But the texts are anonymous and traditional, and this compensates in great measure for their relatively late date: they are the common patrimony of the sacred class of *filid*, trustees and guardians of legendary themes and of forms of art which they hand down from generation to generation.

Less traditionalist and more recent, the literature of Wales also preserves elements of ancient myths in the stories collected under the title *Mabinogion* (tales for recital by apprentice bards? or '*enfances*'?) to which we shall sometimes have to refer in connection with the Irish evidence.

From this ample and diverse collection of documents, with the many verifications which they permit, we may hope to arrive at a presentation neither too arbitrary nor very unfaithful, of the ancient mythology of the Celts. Will this presentation be complete? The investigation of the insular tradition leaves one with a sense of something

[1] See the bibliography, p. 96.

missing. One searches in vain for traces of those vast conceptions of the origin and final destiny of the world which dominate other Indo-European mythologies. Was there a Celtic cosmogony or eschatology? Must we suppose from the few allusions, vague and banal as they are, which Caesar[1] or Pomponius Mela[2] have made to the teaching of the druids, that a whole aspect, and an essential aspect, of this mythical world is hidden from us and will remain hidden? Should we explain the silence of our texts by the censorship of Christian monks, who were nevertheless liberal enough to allow the preservation of episodes much stained with paganism, and features most shocking to the Christian mentality? One may hold an opinion on the matter. In the present state of our knowledge the question cannot be decided. In matters of mythology, as in all historical research, one must sometimes be content with ignorance.

[1]*De Bello Gallico*, vi, 14.
[2]*Chorographia*, iii, 2, 19.

CHAPTER I

THE MYTHOLOGICAL PERIOD

A DISCUSSION of the mythological world of the Celts encounters at once a peculiar difficulty, namely, that when seeking to approach it you find that you are already within. We are accustomed to distinguish the supernatural from the natural. The barrier between the two domains is not, indeed, always impenetrable: the Homeric gods sometimes fight in the ranks of human armies, and a hero may force the gates of Hades and visit the empire of the dead. But the chasm is there nonetheless, and we are made aware of it by the feeling of wonder or horror aroused by this violation of established order. The Celts knew nothing of this, if we are entitled to judge their attitude from Irish tradition. Here there is continuity, in space and in time, between what we call our world and the other world—or worlds. Some peoples, such as the Romans, think of their myths historically; the Irish think of their history mythologically; and so, too, of their geography. Every strange feature of the soil of Ireland is the witness of a myth, and, as it were, its crystallization. The supernatural and the natural penetrate and continue each other, and constant communication between them ensures their organic unity. Hence it is easier to describe the mythological world of the Celts than to define it, for definition implies a contrast.

This omnipresence of the myth in Ireland is specially evident in two collections of stories, the *Dindshenchas* or 'Tradition of Places', which is the mythological geography of the country, and the *Lebor Gabála* or 'Book of Conquests', which is its mythological pre-history. The myths indeed

1

involve both time and space, and the importance of remarkable places, the mystic virtues that belong to them, are
closely bound up with events which happened during the
period when other peoples, human or divine (one can
hardly say exactly which), controlled the land now occupied by the Gaels, but which the Gaels possess only in
partnership with their mysterious forerunners.

This mythological period can be defined as 'a period when
beings lived or events happened such as one no longer sees
in our days'.[1] Christian texts sometimes betray this notion
of a time when other laws than those we know governed
the world. 'In that fight,' says the author of *The Battle of
Mag Tured*, 'Ogma the champion found Orna the sword
of Tethra a king of the Fomorians. Ogma unsheathed the
sword and cleansed it. Then the sword related whatsoever
had been done by it; for it was the custom of swords at
that time, when unsheathed, to set forth the deeds that had
been done by them. And therefore swords are entitled to
the tribute of cleansing them after they have been unsheathed. Hence also charms are preserved in swords thence-
forward. Now the reason why demons used to speak from
weapons at that time was because weapons were worshipped
by human beings then; and the weapons were among the
(legal) safeguards of that time.'[2]

We see that the good cleric does not think of questioning
the truth of a tradition of his time which must have seemed
to him as fanciful as it does to us. At most he feels the need
of explaining it by supposing the intervention of the power
of demons. But how is it that weapons and demons have
lost the power of speech? The scribe who copied the tale
of Cú Chulainn and Fann gives the reason in these closing
words: 'That is the story of the disastrous vision shown to
Cú Chulainn by the fairies. For the diabolical power was

[1] Lévy-Brühl, *La Mentalité Primitive*, 3.
[2] *Revue Celtique*, 12, 107. §. 162.

great before the faith, and it was so great that devils used
to fight with men in bodily form, and used to show
delights and mysteries to them. And people believed that
they were immortal.'[1]

In the same way the stone of Fál, a talisman brought to
Ireland by the ancient gods, whose cry proclaimed the
lawful king of Ireland, is silent to-day, 'for it was a demon
that possessed it, and the power of every idol ceased at the
time of the birth of the Lord.'[2]

We see that Christian Ireland preserved, as a legacy from
paganism, the belief in a time when the supernatural was
natural, when the marvellous was normal. This belief is
indeed characteristic of a mentality common to folklore
('Once upon a time, when animals could speak,' . . .) and
to various so-called 'primitive' peoples. So, in defining the
mythological period, we have borrowed the words used by
Lévy-Bruhl to describe the epoch of the *Dema*, those
ancestral creators who figure in the mythologies of the
natives of New Guinea.

The Book of Conquests is the story of the Irish *Dema*,
retouched, no doubt, by clerics anxious to fit the local
traditions into the framework of Biblical history, while its
pagan quality has not noticeably been altered. We shall
therefore summarize it, according to the texts[3]; and if we
chance to include a secondary episode, it will not matter,
from our present standpoint, provided that it be a product
of the same mythical imagination and suppose the same type
of notion as those elements that are most clearly native.

Tradition has little to say about the first race that inhabited
Ireland, before the Deluge; and we may suspect it to be a
late invention, intended to make up the number of six races
corresponding to the six ages of the world. One of its
leaders was Ladhra, who had sixteen wives and died 'from

[1] LU 4034.
[2] R. A. S. Macalister and J. MacNeill, *Leabhar Gabhála*, 145.
[3] R. A. S. Macalister, *Lebor Gabála Érenn*.

excess of women'. He was the first to die in Ireland. The whole race was destroyed by the Deluge.

Two hundred and sixty-eight years later (Irish annalists are never shy of exactitude) the race of Partholón landed. This name has been explained as a corruption of Bartholomeus,[1] and the legend as a product of the imagination of Christian monks. But whatever be the origin of the name, the mythical character of this personage cannot be doubted, as Van Hamel has shown.[2] He regards Partholón as a god of vegetation; but, apart from the fact that the activities of Partholón extend beyond the domain of agriculture, it is important to observe that here, as throughout the pre-historic tradition, we have to do not with a single god, one mythical individual, but with a whole race, of which Partholón is merely, as it were, a nick-name. It is hard to define this race of Partholón in terms of Indo-European mythology. In the vocabulary of primitive mythology, we may identify it as the first race of those *Dema*, the ancestors (mythical, not human, according to Lévy-Bruhl's useful distinction) who controlled the world, if they did not create it—the world of the Gael, of course, that is to say, Ireland.

When Partholón landed in Ireland, he found there only three lakes and nine rivers, but seven new lakes were formed in his lifetime. He cleared four plains and 'he found no tiller of the soil before him'. He brought with him the steward Accasbél who built the first 'guest-house'; and Brea who built the first dwelling, made the first cauldron and fought the first duel; and Malaliach who was the first surety (guarantee is an essential part of the Celtic legal system), brewed the first beer from bracken, and ordained divination, sacrifice and ritual; Bachorbladhra, who was the first foster-father (fosterage was the basis of the Irish system of education); and finally the two merchants, Biobal, who

[1] R. Thurneysen, ZCP 13, 141; 20, 375.
[2] RC 50, 217.

introduced gold into Ireland, and Babal, who introduced cattle.

It was in Partholón's time that adultery was first committed in Ireland. Having left his wife alone with his servant, he found on his return that they had wronged him. He demanded his 'honour-price', but his wife replied that it was she who was entitled to compensation, for it was the owner's responsibility to protect his property:

> 'honey with a woman, milk with a cat,
> food with one generous, meat with a child,
> a wright within and an edged tool,
> one with one other, it is a great risk'[1]

And this was the first 'judgement' in Ireland. Hence the proverb 'the right of Partholón's wife against her husband.'

The race of Partholón fought the first battle of Ireland against the Fomorians. The name (*Fomoire*) is a compound of the preposition *fo* 'under' and a root which appears in the German *Mahr*, name of a female demon who lies on the breast of people while they sleep (cf. Eng. 'nightmare'), in the name *Morrígan* ('queen of demons'), and perhaps in the name of the formidable Marats of the Veda. The Irish form means 'inferior' or 'latent demons'. The myth presents the Fomorians as native powers constantly driven back to the limits of the world controlled by civilizing races, and always about to invade it and devour its produce. In Partholón's time they had lived for two hundred years in the islands near the coast, 'having no other food'. They fight against Partholón and his people 'with one foot, one hand and one eye', a monstrous form, or a ritual posture (either interpretation seems possible), which has a magic value and a demonic significance. After seven days they are defeated and driven off. But we shall soon see them

[1]*Lebor Gabála*, III, 69; cf. *ibid.* 41.

return, for the Fomorians never lay down their arms. They are like the powers of Chaos, ever latent and hostile to cosmic order.

On the feast of *Beltine*, the First of May, the race of Partholón was destroyed by a mysterious plague; but, by this time, the crafts and institutions by which Celtic society was maintained had already been established. How did this established tradition survive the destruction of the race? How was it transmitted to later peoples? The mythology, naturally incoherent, does not explain.

The race of Nemed, whose name means 'sacred' (cf. Gaul νεμητον 'sacred place'), then occupied Ireland, after the country had lain desert for thirty years. In their time four lakes were formed, two forts were built and twelve plains were cleared. But they were unable to control the Fomorians and finally became their vassals. The land into which Partholón had brought the precious herds of cattle became 'a land of sheep', and every year on the Feast of *Samain*, the First of November, the people of Nemed had to deliver to their masters two-thirds of their corn, their milk and their children. After vain resistance and ruinous victories, they resolved to abandon Ireland.

The race of Partholón was followed by a fourth race, that of the *Fir Bolg*, who arrived on the Feast of *Lugnasad*, the First of August, the third great feast of the Celtic year. Various tribes came with them, *Gaileoin* and *Fir Domnann*, but all were 'only one race and one power'. Unlike their predecessors, these people did not disappear, but left descendants after them. The heroic sagas often mention these elements of the population as distinct from the ruling Gaels.[1] And here the mythology apparently preserves the memory of actual invasions of foreigners. Perhaps the *Gaileoin* are Gauls, the *Fir Domnann* the Dumnonii of Great Britain, the *Fir Bolg* the Belgae. Thus witnesses of a

[1] MacNeill, *Phases of Irish History*, 76.

relatively recent past have come to be introduced between
the fanciful Fomorians and the divine 'Peoples of Dana':
supernatural and human are blended in the crucible of the
myth.

The races of Partholón and Nemed had been clearers of
the plains. With the *Fir Bolg* we seem to emerge from the
era of agrarian culture. No plains are said to have been
cleared in their time, nor any lakes to have been formed.
Their contribution is proper rather to a warlike aristocracy,
for they introduced into Ireland the iron spear-head and the
system of monarchy. It is said of their king Eochaid mac
Eirc that 'no rain fell during his reign, but only the dew;
there was not a year without harvest'. For (we add the
connective on the evidence of several parallel passages)
'falsehood was banished from Ireland in his time. He was
the first to establish there the rule of justice'. Thus there
appears with the establishment of the first Celtic communities in Ireland the principle of association between the king
and the earth—the king's justice being a condition of the
fertility of the soil—which is the very formula of the magic
of kingship.

The *Fir Bolg* were soon to be dispossessed by new invaders, the *Tuatha Dé Danann*, 'Peoples of the Goddess
Dana', who landed on the Feast of *Beltine*, and defeated the
Fir Bolg in the First Battle of Mag Tured. They won the
battle by their 'talent', and this talent consisted of the power
of magic (*draoidheacht*). In distant islands (the 'islands of
Northern Greece') they had learned 'magic and every
sort of craft and liberal art, so that they were learned, wise,
and well skilled in every branch of these arts'. From these
islands they brought four talismans: the Stone of Fál, which
screamed when the lawful king of Ireland placed his foot
upon it; the sword of Nuada, of which the wounds were
fatal; the spear of Lug which gave victory, and the Cauldron
of the Dagda 'from which none parts without being satis-

fied'. To these talismans and to their knowledge of magic, the *Tuatha* owe their supernatural power. They are 'gods' because they are sorcerers. Moreover, among these *Tuatha* only the artisans, those who share this knowledge by which the divine race enjoys its power, are 'gods'. 'They considered their artists to be gods (*dee*) and their labourers to be non-gods (*andee*).' And this distinction recurs in the epic formula: 'the blessing of gods and non-gods upon you!' The divine race, like the human, includes, therefore, in addition to the privileged classes of warriors and initiated craftsmen, a common class which has no share in the magic hierarchy. It is characteristic that this profane element in society is the agricultural class. In this respect the race of the *Tuatha Dé Danann* differs from the preceding races, and in particular from that of Partholón, of which the agrarian character is so marked as to suggest a vegetation myth.

Having conquered the *Fir Bolg*, the *Tuatha Dé Danann* soon came into conflict with the Fomorians, to whom they were opposed in the Second Battle of Mag Tured. This battle, which is the subject of a long epic tale, is one of the dominant episodes of Irish mythology, and one of those most readily susceptible of varying interpretations. Some have found here a conflict between the forces of disorder and darkness and the forces of order and light, a sort of Celtic replica of the struggle of Chthónioi and Ouránioi. And this explanation does account for one aspect, and clearly the dominant aspect, of the rivalry which involved the two races. But we lose perspective by attributing this anarchical conflict of rival peoples to the essential antagonism of opposite cosmic principles; for the two parties were connected by a series of intermarriages so complex as to confuse even the native mythographers, and were forced into opposition by the same play of political events that governs the relations of human beings. In order to illustrate the conditions that govern this mythical world, we shall summarize the origins of the second Battle of Mag Tured.

In the course of a fight with the *Fir Bolg*, Nuada, king of the *Tuatha*, lost an arm. Any mutilation disqualifies a king, so another must be chosen. The chieftains elect Bres ('The Handsome'), who is a son of the king of the Fomorians, but was reared by the *Tuatha* because his mother was one of them. But Bres lacks a sense of what is the first duty of a king, namely generosity. He does not grease the knives of the chieftains, and 'however often they visited them their breath did not smell of beer'. Worse still, he provides neither poets nor musicians nor acrobats nor jesters to entertain them. When their poet presents himself before Bres, he is offered neither bed nor fire, and receives only three dry biscuits on a small dish. Thereupon he pronounced the first satire (*áer*) ever to be pronounced in Ireland, the first of those rhythmic maledictions by means of which the poets, masters of the power of the word, can bring blotches on the face of a prince or sterility upon a whole province:

> 'Without food upon his dish,
> without cow's milk upon which a calf grows,
> without a man's abode under the gloom of night,
> without enough to reward poets, may that be the
> fate of Bres!'[1]

Enraged by his conduct, the chieftains demanded that Bres abdicate, and he invoked the aid of his father, who was king of the Fomorians. Thus the fight is joined, and above the battle of the warriors rages the struggle of wizards on either side who employ every resource of magic and counter-magic. When the five chieftains who constitute the general staff of the *Tuatha* (Nuada, Dagda, Ogma, Goibniu and

[1] RC 12, 70.10=LU 561 [Tr.].

Dian Cécht) decide to declare war, their first care is to mobilize their artisans and make inventory of their magical resources. Their sorcerer promises to hurl against the enemy the twelve mountains of Ireland, their cup-bearer to drain the twelve lakes of Ireland, their druid to cause three showers of fire to rain upon the Fomorians, to deprive them of two-thirds of their valour and strength and to retain the urine of their men and of their horses. Throughout the battle Dian Cécht, the leech, remains, chanting incantations with his three children, beside a well into which the bodies of slain warriors are thrown (for death by violence does not spare the race of gods) and whence they emerge restored to life.

Thus a conflict, arising from the revolt of discontented chieftains, and spreading as a result of the appeal by the dispossessed king to his natural allies (circumstances which reflect in the myth political and domestic conditions familiar to Celtic society) ends in the victory of the divine invaders over the grim Fomorians, who are now finally expelled from the confines of what is to become the domain of the Gael.

The sixth and last race to invade Ireland is that of the 'Sons of Míl', ancestors of the present inhabitants of the country. They landed on the Feast of *Beltine*, and the first three inhabitants that they met were the three eponymous goddesses of Ireland, Éire, Banba and Fódla. The circumstances of the meeting are remarkable. Éire, in welcoming the invaders, predicts that the island will belong to their descendants for ever. The poet Amairgin thanks her, but Donn, the eldest of the Sons of Míl, says rudely: 'It is not you that we must thank, but our gods and our magic powers.' 'What is that to you,' said Éire, 'for neither you nor your children will enjoy this island.' Then she asked of Amairgin that the island should bear her name for ever, and her sisters did likewise; and that is why the island has

three names, Éire, Banba and Fódla. In accordance with
the prophecy of the goddess, Donn was drowned before he
had found a home in Ireland. He was buried on an island
off the west coast, since known as 'The House of Donn'.
The descendants of the Sons of Míl follow him there after
death.[1]

We see how Amairgin secured possession of the country
for his race by conciliating its ancient goddesses, while Donn
failed by his refusal to invoke other gods than his own. This
episode illustrates the attitude of the Celts in religion, a
willingness to adopt local cults and take advantage of the
power that attached to them.

Nevertheless, the Sons of Míl demanded of the *Tuatha*
'combat or sovranty or agreement'. The *Tuatha* gave them
nine days' delay in which 'to depart or to submit or to give
battle.' When they refused, the *Tuatha* appealed to the
judgement of the poets of their adversaries: 'for if they give
an unjust judgement, our elements will kill them on the
spot.' We see that it is the poet, the sacred one, not the
king or the warrior, who appears as arbiter. Amairgin
decided that the Sons of Míl should re-embark and with-
draw 'as far as the ninth wave', that ninth wave which for
the Celts had a magic power. When the invaders sought to
return to shore they were prevented by a 'druidic wind'
raised by the *Tuatha*. (Druidic wind differs from natural
wind in that it blows no higher than the ships' masts.) Then
Amairgin sang an invocation to the great lady Éire:

'I invoke the land of Ireland.
Much coursed be the fertile sea,
    fertile be the fruit-strewn mountain,
    fruit-strewn be the showery wood', etc.[2]

---

[1] Meyer, SPAW 1919, 537.
[2] *Leabhar Gabhála* 257 [Tr.].

The wind abated so that the Sons of Míl were able to land.
As he set his right foot on shore, Amairgin sang again:

> 'I am the wind on the sea.
> I am a wave of the ocean.
> I am the roar of the sea.
> I am a powerful ox.
> I am a hawk on a cliff.
> I am a dewdrop in sunshine.
>
> . . . .
>
> I am the strength of art.
> I am a spear with spoils that wages battle.
>
> . . . .
>
> Who clears the stony place of the mountain?
>
> . . . .
>
> Who has sought peace (in death?) seven times without
>   fear?
>
> . . . .
>
> Who brings his cattle from the house of Tethra?
>
> . . . .
>
> What man, what god forges weapons in a fort? . . .
> Who chants a petition, divides the Ogam letters . . .?
> A wise chanter.'[1]

It has been suggested that this poem, which is a tissue of
obscure formulas that puzzled even the mediaeval com-
mentators, echoes the druidic doctrine of metempsychosis;
but it simply expressed the pride of the sorcerer, whose art
has just brought him triumph over his enemies, and who
now parades his talents and declares his power. For we
know that one of the gifts which all primitive peoples
attribute to their sorcerers is that of shape-shifting.

[1] *Leabhar Gabhála* 263 [Tr.].

These two incantations of Amairgin mark with ritual pathos the solemnity of the moment when man proclaims his sovranty over the earth, by virtue of the magic powers of the poets which have prevailed over the forces opposed to them. They illustrate too the dual attitude of man towards these forces: religion in the invocation, addressed to the eponymous goddess, the local 'Mother', to obtain the fertility of the region of which she is still mistress; and magic in the explosion of pride on the part of the sorcerer who is the embodiment of the art which will enable him to prevail even against the gods. We shall find everywhere amongst the Celts the dialectic of these two attitudes, religion and magic. And if one of the two should be emphasized, it is the second. We have seen that the Irish regarded the gods as master magicians, so that the sacred and the magical are not distinct notions. Their relations with these gods are primarily relations of constraint, only secondarily of deference. We shall observe the same behaviour in the hero, always struggling against the supernatural and seeking to dominate it, to pursue it into its own territory and conquer it with mere weapons.

The Sons of Míl gave battle to the *Tuatha*, killed a great number of them, including the three eponymous goddesses, and put them to flight. The Book of Conquests declares that they were expelled from Ireland. But the common tradition, which is confirmed by modern folklore, contradicts this assertion. Like the *Dema* to whom we have compared them, the *Tuatha* 'returned underground', where they continue to live, in those mounds where the peasant of to-day still believes them to dwell. We must now examine the status of the supernatural after the mythological period comes to an end, and the *modus vivendi* that was established between the two races destined to dwell together upon Irish soil.

CHAPTER II

THE GODS OF THE CONTINENTAL CELTS

WHILE we depend on the witness of the insular Celts for the myths, we have for the images some documents concerning the Celts of the continent. These documents are of two sorts: texts of ancient writers, and Gaulish or Gallo-Roman inscriptions and monuments. The Latin and Greek texts are brief, categorical, and suggest conceptions analogous to those familiar in other mythologies; and therefore they are reassuring. The inscriptions (mere names or epithets of divinities) and the monuments (in so far as they are purely Celtic, for we must reckon with the possibility of Roman influence) give us only allusions which are not easy to interpret and which throw only a little light upon a world of obscure notions. One is tempted to use the texts as a starting-point in order to explain the monuments, and so to fit the fragments of the puzzle into the ready framework that some paragraph of Caesar provides. But this temptation is to be avoided, for it is safer to wander without a guide in an unmapped country than to trust completely a map traced by men who came only as tourists and often with biased judgement. We shall proceed therefore as though no Greek or Roman had ever visited Celtic territory, and examine first the native documents. Then we shall be ready to compare our findings with what other writers have reported.

The first fact that strikes one is the multiplicity of the names of gods, and the fewness of the examples of each of them that occur. According to an early estimate, which is probably not subject to any notable correction, of 374

names attested in the inscriptions 305 occur only once.[1]
The names most frequently mentioned are those of the
gods Grannos (19 times) and Belenos (31 times), and the
goddesses Rosmerta (21 times) and Epona (26 times).
Names of Gaulish gods are legion, and the number has
not been explained by those parallel processes of syncretism
and expansion which elsewhere have resulted in defining
and establishing the features of the gods. In the Gallo-
Roman period, when the native cults became integrated in
the imperial religious system, a single Roman deity represents a multiplicity of local gods whose memory is preserved
in the epithet of the imported foreigner. Thus fifty-nine
different epithets are joined to the name of Mars:[2] Mars
Teutates is the Teutates that we know from Lucan; Mars
Segomo is Segomo whose cult appears in Munster and
whose name occurs in that of the Irish hero Nia Segamon
('Champion of Segomo');[3] Mars Camulus is the disguise
of a god Camulus, identical, no doubt, with Cumall, father
of the hero Finn (s. Chapter VII); Mars Rudianos ('The
Red') recalls the name of the horse-god Rudiobos,[4] for
the horse and the colour red are associated with the land of
the dead and with gods of war throughout Celtic territory.
This is evidenced by the red trappings of the *Morrígan*
and by the three red horsemen from the kingdom of Donn,
lord of the dead, whose appearance in *The Destruction of
Da Derga's Hostel* announces his approaching doom to
king Conaire.[5] Thus a multiplicity of local tribal gods
whom he has supplanted, appears under the unity of the
imperial cult of Mars.

The plurality of names over the whole territory suggests

---

[1] Anwyl, *Trans. Gael. Soc. Inverness*, 26, 411.

[2] Dottin, *Manuel pour servir a l'étude de l'antiquité celtique*, 226.

[3] MacNeill, *Phases of Irish History*, 127.

[4] J. Loth, *Rev. Arch.* 22, 5e Sér. 210; Eva Wunderlich, *Rel.-Geschicht. Versuche*, 20, 46.

[5] RC 22, 36.

that these were tribal gods, the gods of communities or
groups of communities, for their distribution seems to be
political or geographic rather than functional. And this
suggestion is confirmed by a useful observation made by
Vendryes.[1] It is well known that one of the gods most
frequently represented on Gaulish monuments is Tricephalus, a three-headed or three-faced god. We have
thirty-two effigies of him, most of them from Northern
Gaul. Fifteen of the more archaic examples were found in
the territory of the Remi. We may therefore consider
Tricephalus to be a god of the Remi, at least in origin.
Again, the cult of the *Matres* is widespread in the Rhine-
land and especially among the Treviri. But in one instance
we find Tricephalus represented on a stele at Trier, and he
appears surmounted by the three *Matres* of the Treviri who
seem to trample him under foot. This monument may be
compared with a stele discovered at Malmaison, on which
Tricephalus is associated with another group, the pair
consisting of Mercury and his companion Rosmerta. But
here the positions are reversed and Tricephalus seems to
dominate the divine pair. Thus each of the two peoples
has symbolized the triumph of their own god over foreign
or hostile gods. No doubt Vendryes is right in regarding
such evidence as an indication of the national character
that the Remi attributed to their Tricephalus and the
Treviri to their *Matres*.

This tribal character of the god is directly expressed in
the name of a Gaulish god Teutates mentioned by Lucan:
'and those who propitiate with horrid victims ruthless
Teutates, and Esus whose savage shrine makes men shudder,
and Taranis whose altar is no more benign than that of
Scythian Diana'.[2] Teutates has been supposed to be one
of the great Gaulish gods, but this hypothesis is invalidated

---

[1] *Comptes rendus de l'Acad. des Inscriptions*, 1935, 324.
[2] *Bellum Civile*, i, 444–46 (tr. Duff).

by the fact that he is mentioned elsewhere only in a single
inscription, and was adored probably only by some obscure
tribe. The name indeed means simply '(the god) of the
tribe' (G. *touto-*, *teuto-*, Ir. *túath* 'tribe'),[1] a title which corresponds to a familiar formula of Irish sagas: 'I swear by
the god (or gods) by whom my people swear.' Every
Gaulish people had, then, its Teutates, and adored him each
by a different name, or by one of the titles: *Albiorix* 'king
of the world'; *Rigisamus* 'Most Royal'; *Maponos* 'The Great
Youth'; *Toutiorix* 'king of the tribe'; *Caturix* 'king of
battle'; *Loucetius* 'the brilliant one', which are perhaps no
more than means of invoking the god without profaning
his name, by a precaution analogous to that suggested by
the Irish formula. How did these gods of peoples or tribes
appear to the imagination of the Gauls? Without discussing
the effigies in detail, we shall note some general features.[2]

First of all, the triple figures are important, gods with
three heads or three faces and groups of three goddesses.
The number three plays a large part in Celtic tradition; the
'triad', a formula which combines three facts or three
precepts, is a *genre* which dominates the gnomic literature
of both Wales and Ireland, and triple personages or trios
are prominent in the epic tradition of the two peoples.

Another notable fact is the more or less marked zoomorphic character of the effigies, sometimes expressed in a
more evolved form of the same mythological type by
association of an animal with the god. An example is fur-
nished by Cernunnos ('The Horned One'), the god whose
cult is most widely attested. He is represented with the
horns of a ram or a deer, squatting on the ground. The
posture recalls that of the Buddha, but it must have been
habitual to the Gauls, whose furniture did not include any

---

[1] Vendryes, *Teutomatos, Comptes rendus de l'Acad. des Inscriptions*, 1939, 466.
[2] For the images, see W. Krause, *Religion der Kelten* (*Bilderatlas zur Religionsgeschichte*, 17); S. Reinach, *Description raisonnée du musée de Saint-Germain-en-Laye,
Bronzes figurés de la Gaule Romaine*, 137.

sort of chair. He is often accompanied by one or two
horned serpents, and the horned god with a serpent recurs
on the famous Gundestrup vessel. Certain variants present
a female deity, or a three-headed figure, of the same type.

This zoomorphic element appears more clearly in the
female than in the male effigies: one of the most familiar
goddesses is Epona, whose name means 'The Great Mare'
and who appears on horseback accompanied by a mare
with her foal, or feeding some foals; the Welsh Rhiannon,
'The Great Queen', has been recognized as a mare-goddess
comparable to Epona.[1] We find also a bear-goddess, Artio,
and there can be no doubt that the name Damona, formed
like Epona, means 'The Great Cow' (cf. Ir. *dam* 'ox').

These female deities fill a big place in the religious world
of the Gauls. They can be divided into two classes. The
first is that of the tutelary goddesses[2], who are connected
with the earth itself and with local features, wells or forests,
or again with the animals that frequent them, and who
control the fertility of the earth, as is shown by the horn
of plenty which is one of their attributes. Such are the
Matres and Epona and the goddesses of water (Sirona in
eastern Gaul and Brixia, the companion of Luxovius, the
water-god of Luxeuil) or of forests (Dea Arduina of the
Ardennes). The second class, which is smaller, is that of
the goddesses of war: for example, Andarta of the Vocontii,
or Andrasta who was invoked by Boudicca before she went
into battle, or Nemetona whose name resembles that of
Nemain, one of the three *Morrígna* of Irish tradition
(s. p. 32). The two types of which the one represents the
powers of fertility, the other the powers of destruction,
appear separately on continental territory. We find them
confused in the persons of the same divinities in insular
tradition, which represents in this respect, as in others, a

---

[1] H. Hubert, 'Le Mythe d'Epona', *Mélanges Vendryes*, 187.
[2] Daremberg-Saglio, *Dict. des Ant.*, s.v. *Matres*.

less analytical and more archaic conception than the Gaulish.

Many of the goddesses often appear as companions of a god. Brixia and Luxovius have been cited; and Sirona is usually associated with Grannos, sometimes with Apollo; Nemetona appears on the monuments beside Mars, who has, no doubt, been substituted in these cases for some Celtic war-god; Rosmerta is likewise the companion of Mercury. But the pair who appear most frequently are Sucellos and Nantosuelta.

Sucellos, 'The God of the Mallet', whose name means 'Good Striker', has been identified with Dispater, ancestor of the Gauls, of whom Caesar tells us. The appearance of this bearded god, dressed in the short tunic which was the national costume of the Gauls, and expressing strength and authority and, at the same time, a certain benevolence, accords well with one's idea of a father-god, and recalls in many respects the chief god of the Irish, the Dagda (s. Chap. III). His attributes are the mallet, weapon of the 'Good Striker', and the cup or dish, symbol of abundance, and here there is a striking parallel with the two attributes of the Dagda, the club which fells his enemy and the inexhaustible cauldron which ensures abundance to his people. These divinities have, therefore, the two characteristics that define the function of a father-god, who is at the same time a warrior, and therefore protector and nurturer. The name of the companion, Nantosuelta, is obscure, but the first element is recognizable as meaning 'river' (cf. W. *nant* 'stream'). We find, then, on Gaulish soil an association of a father-god with a local river-goddess which is confirmed by an episode of Irish mythology in which the Dagda is associated with the Boyne, the sacred river of Ireland (s. p. 41). Other pairs might be added to this class. In the region of Salzbach a 'god of the mallet' is associated with the goddess Aeracura who appears with

a horn of plenty or a basket of fruit, attributes of the
Matres. In the mythology of the insular Celts we shall find
again these pairs, consisting of the chief god and one of
the *Matres*, and there is no doubt that they present one of
the fundamental notions of Celtic religion.

Tribal gods and mother-goddesses: is it possible to go
beyond this general characterization of the Gaulish divinities? Can one find the trace of a separation of functions
and activities? The attempt has been made on the strength
of a paragraph of Caesar which has been often quoted
and which must again be quoted here. We declined to
begin with this testimony, but it must now be considered.

Caesar uses these words: 'Among the gods they most
worship Mercury. There are numerous images of him;
they declare him the inventor of all arts, the guide for every
road and journey, and they deem him to have the greatest
influence for all money-making and traffic. After him
they set Apollo, Mars, Jupiter and Minerva. Of these
deities they have almost the same idea as other nations:
Apollo drives away diseases, Minerva supplies the first
principles of arts and crafts, Jupiter holds the empire of
heaven, Mars controls wars.'[1]

Thus the great gods of the Celts would seem to correspond more or less exactly to the great gods of the Romans
and would have divided among them, as these do, the
various domains of human activity. Such a coincidence is
a priori surprising. In view of the profound divergence in
mentality and social structure which we observe as between
Romans and Celts, one must wonder at such a similarity in
their religious ideas; and a comparison of this text with the
Gaulish documents confirms the suspicion.

If we consider the goddesses, we have noticed among
the mother-goddesses divinities of water and forest,
goddesses of fertility who protect certain animals, and

[1] *De Bell. Gall.*, vi, 17 (tr. Edwards).

goddesses of war, but nowhere a Minerva, patroness of the arts. This does not mean that some mother-goddess did not play this part. And indeed we shall find a patroness of the arts among the insular Celts in the triple Brigit. Caesar may have observed this quality in some Gaulish goddess unknown to us, or even in one of those we do know but not in this connection. The quality familiar to him, and therefore immediately intelligible, prompted a hasty identification calculated to satisfy him and to mislead us. Caesar's testimony is important inasmuch as it throws light on an aspect of the mother-goddesses which is confirmed by Irish tradition, and about which Gaulish tradition is silent. But by accepting it as it stands we should form a false notion of the complex goddesses of the Celts.

In the case of the gods we are in the same situation. We can well believe that Gaulish gods were warriors, artisans, healers, and that they presided over certain phenomena of the heavens. Which people has not attributed these various activities to its gods? But if we seek, for instance, the contrast between a god of war and a god of arts and crafts, then difficulties arise. This is illustrated by the contradictions of scholiasts who have tried to reconcile the independent evidence of Lucan with the system outlined by Caesar. In a passage cited above Lucan enumerates three gods adored by Gaulish tribes; Teutates, Esus and Taranis. There is nothing to suggest that these are three great Gaulish gods, still less that they are the three principal gods of the Gauls, a conception which, as we have seen, does not correspond to any reality. But in the light of Caesar's testimony, one is led to establish some equivalence between these gods and those that he has defined; and the scholiasts of Lucan have made the attempt.[1] The name Taranis, which means 'Thunderer' (cf. Ir. *torann* 'thunder') indicates an identification with Jupiter. But, as between Esus and

[1] *Commenta Bernensia*, ed. Usener, 32.

Teutates, which corresponds to Mars and which to Mercury? There is so little correspondence that the two scholiasts have answered the question in contradictory terms, so that we find both Esus and Teutates identified with each of the two Roman gods. We have seen that in fact Teutates is simply 'the god of the tribe'; and he must have been regarded sometimes as a god of war and sometimes as a god of industry, according as he was invoked in times of war or peace. No doubt it was the same in the case of Esus, whose name may mean 'master', if the comparison with Latin *erus* be correct.[1] Lucan describes him as the blood-thirsty master of warlike tribes, but on the altars of Trier and Paris he appears as the gracious patron of a peaceful corporation of builders.[2] Similarly the Irish Lug is an artisan of many talents, even a healer, but also a warrior whose spear never misses its mark. General and complete efficiency is the character of all the Celtic gods, and we see them fighting or giving help and counsel, according to the needs of their people.

However, there is one point in the testimony of Caesar which must be remembered, and it requires interpretation. It is the pre-eminence that he accords to the Gaulish Mercury over the other gods, including the lord of heaven. This conflicts so strongly with the notions that were familiar to him that we are bound to accept it; and, moreover, it is confirmed by insular tradition. But we must not rush to the conclusion that the Gauls distinguished a god of arts and crafts as opposed to a god of war, and preferred one to the other. The cult of Mars, who is adored under fifty-nine different titles, is no less widespread in Gallo-Roman Gaul than that of Mercury, who possesses only nineteen titles. We must rather suppose that the Gauls gave precedence in their divine world to the craftsman

---

[1] Ernout and Meillet, *Dict. Etym. de la langue latine* (2nd ed.), 310.
[2] St. Czarnowski, RC 42, 1.

over the warrior, and that both qualities could be combined, and were normally combined, in one divine person. This, at least, is how we should explain, in terms of Celtic mythology, the fact which impressed Caesar, and which he explained in Roman terms.

Some general characteristics have emerged from this rapid survey: the multiplicity of divine persons, sometimes in triple form, sometimes in animal form; tribal character, marked in the case of the gods; local character, especially in the case of the goddesses; the importance of female deities, goddesses of war or mother-goddesses; the frequent association of these females with tribal gods; the lack of differentiation of functions as among the gods; and the importance of the craftsman in the celestial hierarchy. These characteristics appear only as shadows in our picture of the religious world of the Gauls, for our imperfect knowledge permits merely a sketch; but we shall observe them again, more clearly drawn, and emphasized by the rich colour of a living mythology, in the epic tradition of the insular Celts.

CHAPTER III

THE MOTHER-GODDESSES OF IRELAND

IT is a remarkable fact that the relative importance of gods and goddesses in Irish mythology varies considerably according to the documents that one examines. In the 'historical' tradition which has been summarized in the first chapter, the principal role belongs to colonizers, inventors or male warriors, and female persons intervene only in episodes. On the other hand, in the 'geographical' tales of the *Dindshenchas* the female divinities fill a much larger place. This is explained by what has already been observed from Gaulish evidence, namely, the national or tribal character of the gods and the local character of the goddesses. It is not an accident that the former dominate the historical myths and the latter the topographical myths.

Without attempting to collect all the myths concerning the many goddesses of Ireland, we shall notice some facts which are characteristic of the chief qualities presented by these deities.

To the earliest stratum of tradition belong some persons of whom the literature has but little to say. Only a few scattered references reveal their names and their function. They are the mothers of the gods. Anu, or Ana, *mater deorum hibernensium*, 'nurtures well the gods' according to Cormac the Glossator. Munster owes its fertility to Anu, goddess of prosperity, and she is adored there: the 'Two Paps of Anu' in that province are called after her.[1] Anu has been more or less confused with Danu, or Dana, from whom the *Tuatha Dé Danann* ('Tribes of the goddess Dana')

---

[1] *Cóir Anmann*, § 1 (Stokes and Windisch, *Irische Texte*, iii, 289).

take their name; and these are sometimes called merely *Tuatha Dé*, 'Tribes of the Goddess', as though she is the goddess *par excellence*.

To the same class as Anu and Danu belongs the other goddess *par excellence*, namely the triple Brigit—or perhaps there were three sisters Brigit—who is adored by poets, smiths and leeches.[1] She survives to-day in the Christian saint Brigid, who is for the Irish the most excellent saint, just as the pagan Brigit was the most excellent goddess. The saint has faithfully preserved the character of the goddess: being a mother-goddess, she watches over childbirth, and modern folklore makes her the midwife of the Blessed Virgin; as goddess of prosperity, she brings abundance to the country hearths which she visits, leaving her footprint in the ashes; as seasonal goddess, she has her feast on the day of the great pagan feast of purification, *Imbolc*, the First of February; and finally, as triple goddess, she is propitiated by the sacrifice of a fowl buried alive at the meeting of three waters.[2] Thus the cult of these great goddesses manifests its endurance. Religions succeed one another, gods die and are forgotten, but the peasant of the Highlands still, after thousands of years, continues to honour with a humble ritual those powers more ancient than the gods.

One might ask whether Anu, Danu and Brigit, these 'mothers' who resemble each other so closely, are really distinct deities or merely different names for the same person. I think that in this form the question is meaningless. We must dismiss the notion of one deity who is titular, as it were, of a particular function, in favour of the notion of diverse realizations of a single religious idea, groups of deities, probably local—at least in origin—who are not identical but equivalent, having evolved among different

[1] J. O'Donovan, *Cormac's Glossary*, 23.
[2] A. Carmichael, *Carmina Gadelica*, i, 168.

peoples, perhaps at different times, from the same generative
impulse. We shall find at every point of the epic tradition
similar figures as mothers and teachers, no longer gods
but heroes: Buanann ('The Lasting One'), 'Mother and
nurse of heroes';[1] Scáthach ('The Shadowy One') to whom
Cú Chulainn goes to complete his training as a warrior, and
who reveals to him the secrets that make him invincible
(s. Chap. VI).

Another group of deities illustrates complementary
aspects of the same type, namely the seasonal goddesses,
patronesses of the great feasts of Ireland and of the sacred
places where these feasts are celebrated: Macha, or rather
the Machas, Carman, Tailtiu, Tea and others.

Tradition distinguishes various Machas, eponyms of the
Plain of Macha, of the Citadel of Macha (Emain Macha,
capital of pagan Ulster), of the Hill of Macha (Ard Macha,
metropolis of Christian Ireland), and patronesses of the
Assembly of Macha which was held at the time of the
feast of *Lugnasad*, the First of August. They form a series
from the most ancient mythical pre-history down to the
beginning of the Christian era, from Macha, wife of
Nemed, leader of the third race to inhabit Ireland, to
Macha, wife of the peasant Crunnchu, who was a contemporary of king Conchobor. And it is certainly not an
accident that they bear the name of the warrior-goddess,
one of the three *Morrígna*. To what degree are these
personages originally distinct one from another, and different from the warrior-goddess? In what measure are
they to be explained as secondary developments, as myths
invented to explain some obscure rite which was a vestige
of the cult of some goddess of the past? From our point
of view it does not matter much. What does matter is
that for a long time the imagination of the Celts persisted
in gathering around a particular feast, or a particular place,

[1] O'Donovan, *Cormac's Glossary*, 17.

or a particular complex of ritual, a given type of mythological symbolism.

The characteristics of a goddess of fertility, who presides over the rites of childbirth, are clearly recognizable in the myth of Macha, the wife of Crunnchu.[1] One day Crunnchu, a rich peasant widower, sees a beautiful young woman come into his house. She says nothing but at once sets about the duties of the house. Having gone around the room in the ritual manner, clockwise, she goes into his bed. She becomes pregnant by him, and from that day everything prospers in the house. The time comes when Crunnchu must go to attend the provincial assembly of Ulster, and Macha warns him not to mention her name there. But when he sees the king's horses racing, Crunnchu, forgetting the prohibition, exclaims that his wife is swifter than they are. King Conchobor accepts the challenge and orders that the woman be brought to race against his horses. In vain Macha asks for a delay since her time is at hand. She must accept the ordeal or see her husband put to death. Undoing her hair, she enters the race and reaches the post before the horses; but then she cries out and dies, giving birth to twins, 'The Twins of Macha', in Irish *Emain Macha*, from whom the capital of Ulster is named. Before she dies she curses the men of Ulster and predicts that for nine times nine generations they shall suffer the sickness of childbirth in the height of war and in the hour of greatest danger. This is the origin of the 'Novena of the Ulsterman', that curse which afflicted all the males of the province for five nights and four days. Another story explains it differently: after Cú Chulainn had lived for a year with the fairy Fedelm of the Long Hair, she appeared naked before the men of Ulster, and, from the sight, they were afflicted with this strange disease.[2]

[1] Thurneysen, *Heldensage*, 361.
[2] Thurneysen, *op. cit.*, 359.

But through the different versions there appears the constant relation between the curse and a goddess who was
the spouse of a mortal.

The ethnological significance of this 'novena' has been
discussed by scholars,[1] and the question raised as to whether
it is a form of the *couvade* practised by various primitive
peoples, who impose upon the husband of a woman in
childbirth the same seclusion and the same precautions as
upon the mother. The 'novena' differs from the *couvade*
in that the men are subject to it not as individuals, when a
child is born to them, but collectively. It is clearly a
collective rite, a symbolic mime in honour of the mother-
goddess; and the myth of Macha supplies also the explanation of another rite, namely the women's races which were
a special feature of the Assembly of Emain. The fact that
the rite of childbirth is attached, not to the day of the
feast, but to a time of war is anomalous, and calls for
explanation. Perhaps it was indeed a resource employed
'in the hour of greatest danger' in order to propitiate the
Mother-Goddess, who would then appear to have been a
protectress in war as in peace. The warlike character of
another Macha makes this view probable.

At that time, the story says,[2] three kings, Dithorba, Áed
and Cimbáeth, reigned alternately in Ireland, each for seven
years. Áed died, leaving a daughter, Macha The Red, but
when her turn came, Cimbáeth and Dithorba refused to
entrust the royal power to a woman. She gave them
battle and put them to flight, and reigned for seven years.
Meanwhile Dithorba died, leaving five sons, and they, in
due course, claimed the kingdom from Macha. But she
refused on the ground that she held it not by right of
inheritance but by right of conquest, and she conquered
the sons as she had conquered the father. Macha then

---

[1] Vendryes, *Comptes rendus de l'Acad. des Inscript.*, 1934, 329.
[2] *The Rennes Dindshenchas*, § 611 (RC 16, 281).

married the other royal claimant Cimbáeth, and made him chief of her mercenaries. She visited the five sons of Dithorba in the guise of a leper. They were seated around a camp fire eating boar's flesh, and she ate with them. Then one of them said: 'The woman (*cailleach*, which is to this day the word for a local goddess) has beautiful eyes. Let us lie with her.' And he brought her into the forest. She bound him then by force and returned alone to the fire. 'Where is he that went with you?' asked the brothers. 'He is ashamed to return to you,' she said, 'after lying with a leper.' 'There is no shame in that,' said they, 'for we should all do as much.' She led them into the forest one by one, and bound them all. Then, having reduced them to slavery, she made them build the rampart of the future capital, Emain Macha.

In the person of this second Macha we discover a new aspect of the local goddess, that of the warrior and domi-nator; and this is combined with the sexual aspect in a specific manner which reappears in other myths, the male partner or partners being dominated by the female.

Going farther back in time, we encounter Macha, the wife of Nemed, of whom we are told only that she died in the plain of Macha which her husband had cleared, and which he 'bestowed upon his wife so that it might bear her name.'[1] This third eponym appears as an agrarian deity, companion of one of the mythological ancestors, one of the *Dema*, of Ireland.

We shall see in the case of other goddesses, associated with other sacred places or other feasts, these different elements of which the three Machas present various com-binations: the maternal reproductive element, which pre-dominates in Macha, wife of Crunnchu; the agrarian element (which is merely another aspect of the first, since

[1] *ibid.* § 94 (RC 16, 45).

the notion of fertility is the same) in the wife of Nemed
and also in the wife of the farmer, Crunnchu, who belongs
to the peasant class which the *Tuatha* treated as an un-
initiate crowd (p. 8); the warlike element, compounded
with the sexual, in the daughter of Áed.

The feast of *Lugnasad*, which in Ulster was held at Emain
Macha, was held in Leinster at Carman and at Tailtiu.
Tailtiu owes its name to Tailtiu, daughter of Mag Mór
('Great Plain') of the race of *Fir Bolg*. After the defeat
of this race by the *Tuatha Dé Danann* and the death of
her husband, she became the wife of a chief of the *Tuatha*
With an axe, she cleared all Ireland 'where she was held
in captivity'. Thus she made of the forest-covered region
of Breg a plain 'all covered with clover'. She died from
the exhaustion of this effort. The men of Ireland sang a
lament for her, and her foster-son, the god Lug, established the feast of Tailtiu in her honour. This feast lasts
for a month, fifteen days before *Lugnasad* and fifteen days
afterwards. As long as it shall continue to be held, there
will be 'corn and milk in every house, peace and fair
weather for the feast'. Even St. Patrick himself respected
this ancient pagan tradition. 'Victorious was the proud
law of nature; though it was not made in obedience to
God, the Lord was magnifying it.'[1]

Carman, 'leader of an army in many battles', was the
mother of three sons, 'The Fierce, The Black and the
Wicked'. The four of them devastated Ireland, the mother
by her sorcery which 'destroyed the juice of nourishing
fruits', and the sons by plundering, until they were defeated by the *Tuatha Dé Danann*. The sons were compelled to depart from Ireland, leaving their mother as a
hostage, and 'the seven things (amulets?) which they
worshipped'. Carman died of grief in her captivity, asking
that a feast should be held in her honour for ever.

[1] E. J. Gwynn, *The Metrical Dindshenchas*, iv, 153.

Other 'goddesses of feasts' are Tea, patroness of the Assembly of Tara, who was 'held in captivity', according to tradition, like Tailtiu and Carman; and Tlachtga, who bore three sons at a single birth, each by a different father, and died, like Macha, in giving them birth. All the great assemblies of Ireland are thus placed under the invocation of local deities, mothers, clearers of plains, mistresses of the fruits of the earth, which they bestow in plenty when propitious, or, when hostile, they destroy. Survivors of races anterior to the race of men, and even to the race of the gods, they are often imagined as held in captivity by the actual possessors of the soil who have had to overcome them by violence before conciliating them by ritual means. They are personifications of the powers of nature, earthy forces, which man must conquer in order to make them serve him.

We know only those goddesses who presided over the great provincial assemblies and have thus found a place in the literary and aristocratic tradition. Probably more numerous were those whose cult was limited to certain rural communities and has left no trace. The name of one of these has come down to us by chance, that of Mongfhinn, the sorceress, who died on the eve of *Samain*, and to whom, as an old Ossianic tale says, 'the women and common people address their prayers'.[1] It is an instance of the preservation of one of these ancient conservative cults by the less cultivated classes, while they have fallen into the background of the epic tradition, ousted by the prestige of the great male gods.

We have seen that some of the mother-goddesses appear also as warriors; and there is a group in whom this warlike character is dominant. The goddesses of war are imagined as forming a trio, a notion which survives on British territory in the dedication of the Benwell inscription *Lamiis*

---

[1] O'Grady, *Silva Gadelica*, ii, 375.

Tribus ('to the Three Lamii').[1] The persons of the trio
are not always the same. The *Badb* ('Crow') and the
Morrígan ('Queen of Phantoms') are accompanied sometimes by *Nemain* ('Panic') and sometimes by Macha.
Nemain and the *Badb* also occur as wives of the ancient
war-god *Nét*, and their names appear in the plural as terms
for the group of three sisters (*Morrígna*) or for supernatural
beings who haunt the battlefield (*Badba*).

It is remarkable that the gods of slaughter have been
personified as women in Irish mythology. The epic tradition knows no equivalent for Ares or Mars; the god Nét
plays no part in it and is scarcely more than a name to
us. There are plenty of fighting gods; indeed all the gods
of the Celts are fighters. But these goddesses of war are
not necessarily fighters. While the Dagda, Lug or Nuada
wield the club or the spear or the sword, the *Morrígna* and
the *Badba* reign over the battlefield, 'the garden of the
Badb', without having to join in the fray. Or, if they do
take part, they need not strike a blow in order to confound
an army. *The Cattle-Raid of Cualnge* says: 'Nemain,
that is the *Badb*, caused confusion in the army so that the
four provinces of Ireland massacred each other with their
own spears and their own weapons, and that a hundred
warriors died of terror and heart-failure that night.'[2] On
the eve of the battle of Mag Tured, the *Morrígan* promised
her help to the Dagda. But it was magic, not military
help: she would deprive the enemy leader of 'the blood of
his heart and the kidneys of his courage', like the Australian
sorcerer who removes from his victim 'the fat of his loins'.
And before the battle she sends her allies two handfuls of
blood.[3] Even when the goddess is induced to take part
directly in the fight, it is not in the guise of a warrior that

[1] CIL, vii, 507.
[2] Thurneysen, *Heldensage*, 177.
[3] RC 12, 85.

she attacks the hero Cú Chulainn.[1] She comes as an eel which winds itself round his legs while he fights at the ford, or as a wolf driving frightened herds of cattle against him, or as a red cow without horns. Thus wherever the *Morrígan* appear in warfare it is by some mystical influence, or by sorcery, or in some animal disguise. These war-goddesses are not warriors. They leave the use of weapons to the divine combatants, to the gods of the tribe. Indeed they have no weapons. It is noteworthy that the two descriptions in the sagas of the equipment of the *Badb* and of the *Morrígan* mention chariot, horse and clothing, but no weapons, whereas in the case of warriors, the description of weapons is one of the favourite common-places. The goddesses in whom the destructive and in-human powers of slaughter are personified contrast in this respect with gods who preside over warfare as a human activity, an art and a profession. It is a symmetrical opposi-tion, even more rigorous than the opposition between mother-goddesses as personifications of fertility and the great ancestral farmers and artisans. Thus for production and destruction, in peace as in war, a double principle is in balance, the female governing the natural event, the male governing the social event.

We have had occasion to mention the animal trans-formations of the *Morrígan*. This zoomorphism is an important feature of many Irish goddesses, while the gods present only some feeble traces of it. Lug is perhaps a raven-god in origin,[2] but nowhere in Irish mythology does this quality appear. On the other hand, the *Badb Catha* ('Raven of Battle') appears to the hero Cú Chulainn in the form of a crow, and likewise the *Morrígan* comes in the form of a bird and alights beside the Bull of Cuailnge

---

[1] Thurneysen, *op. cit.*, 172.
[2] A. H. Krappe, *Revue de l'histoire des religions*, 114, 236.

to incite him with a prophetic incantation.[1] By their triple nature and by this semi-animal nature, the Irish goddesses are related to the types of deity that we encountered among the continental Celts, and reveal a mentality more archaic than that which finds expression in the persons of the male gods who are clearly anthropomorphic and simple, that is to say, not in groups of three.

These goddesses of war sometimes appear in association with an anonymous male companion. The motif is obscure, but other mythological themes perhaps provide the explanation of its significance. One of the most striking descriptions occurs in the episode of the meeting between Cú Chulainn and the *Badb* already cited.

One day Cú Chulainn is suddenly awakened by a cry so terrible that he, the fearless hero, falls out of his bed in alarm. He rushes out naked in his confusion, and his wife Emer has to pursue him, bringing clothes and weapons. He mounts his chariot and sets out in the direction from which the cry was heard. He sees a chariot approaching, to which a single red horse is harnessed. This nightmare horse has only one leg (sorcerers often have one hand and one foot, s. pp. 5, 78); the chariot-pole passes through its body and is held by a peg in the middle of its forehead. In the chariot is a red woman with red eyebrows and a long red cloak down to the ground. Beside the chariot goes a man bearing a fork of hazel (a tree which has magic properties), and driving a cow. Cú Chulainn, who is the guardian of the cattle of the province, protests against the theft of the cow. The woman gives him an answer. 'Why does not the man answer?' asks the hero. 'That is not a man', says the woman. 'He is certainly not a man,' says Cú Chulainn, 'since it is you who answer me'. He then asks the strangers' names, and they answer in an unintelligible rigmarole the terms of which are vaguely threatening:

[1] Thurneysen, *op. cit.*, 144.

'cold wind'; 'cutting'; 'terror'. Finally in exasperation at the woman's sarcasms, the hero leaps on to the chariot, but everything disappears and there is left only a black bird, the *Badb*.

In other stories we find this same pair with even more demoniacal attributes. An example is the adventure of king Conaire in *The Destruction of Da Derga's Hostel*: he meets a man with one arm, one eye, and one leg, armed with an iron fork, and carrying on his back a roast pig which is still squealing. He is accompanied by a woman with a huge mouth, whose pudenda hang down to her knees. A similar monstrous woman comes that night to ask the king for hospitality, and, when asked her name, she recites 'on one foot and one hand' a litany of thirty-one names, including *Badb, Macha* and *Noínden* ('Novena') the name of the curse inflicted upon the men of Ulster by the malediction of Macha.[1] The sexual character of the *Badb*, and her connection with a rite of childbirth, provide the link between the mother-goddesses and the goddesses of war.

This diabolical pair reappear in Welsh tradition, in the *Mbanogi* of Branwen which elsewhere betrays strong Irish influence. The king of Ireland tells how one day he saw emerge from the Lake of the Cauldron a huge man of gross appearance carrying a cauldron, and accompanied by a woman twice as big. The cauldron was a cauldron of resurrection: if a dead man were thrown into it, he came out alive but deprived of speech. The woman was pregnant and was to bear a man fully armed in childbed.[2] This couple, consisting of a mother-goddess, who combines warlike and sexual qualities, and a companion bearing in one instance a fork, in the other a cauldron, belongs to the same class as the couples which consist of the Gaulish

[1] Thurneysen, *op. cit.*, 635, 639.
[2] J. Loth, *Mabinogion*, i, 129, 130.

god with the mallet and Nantosuelta, or the Dagda with
his club and his cauldron and the *Morrígan* (s. Chapter IV).
It presents an even earlier state of tradition, as is shown
by the predominance of the goddess over her male companion, which reflects a matriarchal notion in conflict with
the social order of Celtic communities in historic times.
This is evidenced by the scandal caused to Cú Chulainn by
the conduct of the *Badb* in the episode cited.

The mythological motif in question explains one of the
strangest personages of heroic tradition, namely Queen
Medb, warlike spouse of a comparatively negligible husband, Ailill, king of Connaught.   An ancient deity has
been identified beneath the quasi-historical features of this
Irish Boudicca.[1]   The mere fact that there is a sacred tree
of Medb (*Bile Medba*) is in itself significant.   And, moreover, some of the most characteristic features of the mother-
goddesses can be traced in her whom the poet calls the
'queen-wolf', the sight of whom deprives men of two-
thirds of their strength, and who, like Macha, outruns
horses on the track.[2]   The text entitled 'The Number of
Medb's husbands'[3] lists the different husbands, whom,
kings as they are, this imperious person reduces to the rank
of mere confederates.   One of her companions presents
strongly marked mythological traits.   He is Fergus, her
lover, whose name means 'virility' and who is also called
Ro-ech ('great horse').   He eats seven times as much as
an ordinary man, he has the strength of seven hundred
men, his nose, his mouth and his penis are seven fingers in
length, his scrotum is as big as a sack of flour.   He needs
no less than seven women when separated from his wife
Flidais.   Flidais is a woodland deity and travels in a chariot
drawn by deer.   She reigns over the beasts of the forest

---

[1] Thurneysen, ZCP 18, 108.
[2] E. J. Gwynn, *Metr. Dindsh.*, iv, 367.
[3] Thurneysen, *Heldensage*, 531.

'the herds of Flidais', as Tethra reigns over the creatures of the sea, 'the herds of Tethra'.[1] Just as Nét, the war-god, has two companions, Nemain and Badb, it seems that Fergus has two partners, Flidais the forester and Medb the warrior.

The personality of Medb represents in the euhemerized literary tradition the complete type of a deity who is at the same time a mother and a warrior. We find the completion of this same type in popular tradition in the redoubtable *cailleacha* ('old women') who haunt the countryside in Ireland and Scotland, and to whom the *mamau* ('mothers') of Wales correspond. It is not our purpose to pursue the development of these mythical figures in modern folklore,[2] but it is necessary to point out the persistent vitality of a notion which is deeply rooted in Celtic soil.

Scholars have noted the absence of a Celtic goddess of love, equivalent to Venus or Aphrodite. This lacuna has been explained in unexpected ways, as due to the chastity of the Celt or to the predominance of the maternal element over the amorous.[3] But the comprehensive and undifferentiated activity of Celtic deities that we have observed shows that the impression of a lacuna is illusory. Most of the Celtic goddesses show more or less marked sexual character. To wonder that we do not find a goddess presenting this character to the exclusion of all others is to judge Celtic mythology by foreign standards, and so to condemn oneself to a misconstruction of its intimate system.

[1] Thurneysen, *Heldensage*, 318.
[2] A. H. Krappe, 'La Cailleach Bhéara', *Etudes Celtiques*, i, 292.
[3] J. Weisweiler, ZCP 21, 219.

CHAPTER IV

THE CHIEFTAIN-GODS OF IRELAND

W<small>E</small> have seen that the Irish imagined their gods as forming groups similar to the family-groups which are the basis of Celtic society, *tuatha* ('tribes') placed under the invocation of a mother-goddess Dana. Certain strongly individualized persons stand out from these groups as chieftain-gods of the *Tuatha*: the Dagda, Lug, king Nuada, who are seconded by the champion Ogma, the smith Goibniu, the leech Dian Cécht, and a whole company of magicians and craftsmen. We shall consider here only two of these figures, chosen because they represent two distinct notions and doubtless two different moments of the religious thought of the Celts. These are the Dagda and Lug.

The god who is ordinarily known as the Dagda is also called Eochaid Ollathair, Eochaid 'Father of All' or 'Supreme Father'. This epithet does not mean that he is in fact the father of all the other gods; we know from the genealogies that he is not. It expresses merely the paternal character inherent to the notion of chieftain in a patriarchal society, where the chieftain's power is felt to be of the same nature as that of the father, being, at least in theory, the extension and transposition on the political plane of a father's power in the family. The *Dagda*, literally the 'Good God' is not a name but a title, and an episode of the *Battle of Mag Tured* enables us to establish its exact meaning. At the council of war held by the gods of the *Tuatha*, each one announced what he proposed to do in the common cause. When the Dagda's turn came he said: 'All that you promise to do I shall do myself alone. "You are the good god", said they, and from that day he was called the Dagda.'[1] We see that the adjective has no moral import, but has rather the value that we give it when we say that someone is 'good at' something. And indeed the Dagda is good at everything. He is not only first among magicians; he is a formidable fighter. Under his club the bones of warriors are 'like hailstones under the hooves of horses'. He is an artisan who builds fortresses for the Fomorians, when their king, Bres, has reduced the *Tuatha* to vassalage. His superiority rests in this omnipotence which derives from his omniscience. And his omniscience is expressed in another of his titles, *Ruad Ro-fhessa* ('Lord of Perfect Knowledge'), 'for it is he that had the perfection of the heathen science, and it is he that had the multiform triads'.[2]

The figure of the chieftain-father bears the stamp of a primitive style which redactors have deliberately pressed to a grotesque extreme. Hideous and pot-bellied, he wears a cowl and a short tunic like that of the Gaulish god of the mallet; but in Irish sagas long garments are a measure of the dignity of the wearer, and this tunic is the ordinary attire of churls. His boots are of horse-hide with the hair outside, like the shoes of raw hide still worn to-day by the fishermen of the western islands. The enormous club, mounted on wheels, which he drags along, is so heavy that eight men would be required to carry it, and its track in the ground is as deep as the dyke which marks the frontier of two provinces. With one end of the club he can kill nine men; with the other he restores them to life.[3] Lord of life and death by means of this magic club, he is also lord of abundance by means of his inexhaustible

[1] RC 12, 82. § 81.
[2] *Cóir Anmann*, § 152 (*Irische Texte*, iii, 357).
[3] RC 12, 87. § 93; Thurneysen, *Heldensage*, 479.

cauldron, from which 'no one goes away without being satisfied'. We have had occasion to notice the analogy between these two attributes and the wooden fork and the cauldron of the companion of the mother-goddesses on the one hand, and the mallet and purse, or horn, of plenty of the Gaulish Sucellos on the other. The Dagda reminds one indeed of the god of the mallet. Not that he is the same person, but he belongs in some degree to the same type, and he is an independent but comparable realization of the same notion of a chieftain-god, being both a 'good striker' (*Su-cellos*) and a nurturer.

This barbarous power, which manifests itself in battle in the killer, is manifest under an orgiastic form in an episode of great mythological significance in the story of the Battle of Mag Tured.[1] The Dagda went, during the period of the feast of *Samain,* into the camp of his adversaries, the Fomorians. They made him a porridge 'for he was a great eater of porridge'. They filled the king's cauldron, which held twenty measures of milk and as many more of flour and fat. And into it they put goats and sheep, halves of pork and quarters of lard; and the whole mixture was boiled. Then it was poured into a hole dug in the ground (as is still done to-day on the day of *Samain* with the food offered to the spirits), and Indech, leader of the Fomorians, ordered the Dagda to eat it all under pain of death. The Dagda took his ladle, which was 'so big that a man and a woman could have lain together in it'; and not content with eating the whole meal, he scraped the hole with his finger and ate even the gravel at the bottom. The ordeal thus imposed upon the Dagda recalls those which are imposed periodically and ritually by a people upon their chief. In ancient China, during the drinking-bout of the long night, 'the king, who must show his ability by various exploits, must prove it above all by filling

[1] RC 12, 85. § 89.

himself as tight as a water skin.'[1] After the feast the Dagda has intercourse with his enemy's daughter, not without difficulty, for his stomach is greatly distended, and she promises in return to serve him against her father with her magic powers. While the redactors delighted in emphasizing the grotesque obscenity of this double episode, one can recognize it as a ritual manifestation of the powers of voracity and sexual vigour which are attributes necessary to the prestige of a barbarous chieftain.

Another episode, no doubt a doublet of the former and, also connected with the feast of *Samain*, is even more explicit. The Dagda has a rendezvous with a woman. He finds her by the river Unius in Connaught, in the act of washing, 'with one foot south of the water and one foot north of the water'. Nine loose tresses hang about her head. They have intercourse, and the place is called 'The Bed of the Couple' ever since. This woman was the *Morrígan*. She warns him of the plans of his enemies and promises her aid in the battle.[2]

Thus the chieftain-god is united on a ritual date with a goddess whose protection he thus wins for his people. Is she a mother-goddess or a goddess of war? We have seen that no clear line can be drawn between these two. Here the *Morrígan* is associated with a river, and we are reminded of another motif of the myth of the Dagda, namely his union with Boann,[3] wife of Nechtán (who is doubtless a god of the waters), and eponym of the sacred river, the Jordan of Ireland. The pair prolong the night for nine months, so that when day breaks a son, Aongus, is born, whose name means 'unique force', and who is also called *Mac in Dá Óc*, 'the son of the two young ones'.

---

[1] M. Granet, *La Civilisation chinoise*, 239. It is noteworthy that this winter drinking-bout took place at a period which marked the limit between the successive years (*ib.* 237), a position corresponding to that of the night of Samain.

[2] RC 12, 85.

[3] Thurneysen, *Heldensage*, 605.

This title cannot be justified if we understand 'young' as referring to the real age of the parents, for the Dagda is certainly not young in this sense. It must allude to the eternal youth of the pair, chieftain-god and mother-goddess, whose ritual union at this date of *Samain*, when the Celtic year is born, is the guarantee of the ever renewed vitality of the tribe, being a symbol of the union between the tribe, represented by its chief, and the river-goddess who fertilizes its territory. This sexual element which is so marked in the myth of the Dagda is illuminated by a comparison with the hierogamic rite practised by the king of an Ulster tribe, not with a river-goddess but with a mare, the incarnation of some animal goddess, some Epona, and merely another type of mother-goddess (s. pp. xv, 19) These pairs are analogous to the pair consisting of Sucellos, the 'good striker', and his companion, the river-goddess Nantosuelta.

The figure of the Dagda in its essential features is thus clearly defined. A chieftain-god, he is regarded as the father of his people, by his knowledge their chief magician, by his club—a primitive weapon whose purpose has been forgotten in the sagas—their defender, by his cauldron their nurturer. His orgies of food are at the same time demonstrations of vitality and a ritual of plenty. By his periodic unions with the deities of the earth, he ensures their protection for his people and consecrates in his person the union of earth and man. We have here a mythico-ritual complex which belongs to the most ancient deposit that Irish tradition has preserved.

The figure of the god Lug appears to be the product of religious ideas that are less archaic, and of a more advanced culture. But it derives from common Celtic sources, and the correspondences that can be identified, as between one people and another, make it possible to trace some primitive elements. The name of the god, which may mean 'crow',

and the fact that this bird figures in the armorial bearings
of the city of Lyons, Lugudunum (fortress of Lug) are
evidence of the zoomorphic character that we have observed in the Gaulish gods and the mother-goddesses.[1] The
continental inscriptions dedicated to the *Lugoues*, and
certain Irish legends which mention two brothers of Lug,
bearing the same name, who died in early youth, reveal
the triple form frequent in these deities. But the legend
of the god has eliminated these two features. While the
goddesses have preserved something of the 'fluidity' (to
borrow the term used by Lévy-Bruhl) that characterizes a
primitive world in which the limits of individual and species
are not yet fixed, the male gods belong to a more advanced
system of imagery in which the principle of identity is
more rigorously applied, so that even a mythical figure
is no longer imagined as at once simple and triple, animal
and man.

Lug is functionally a chieftain-god like the Dagda; but
he is in contrast to the Dagda in many respects. He is the
product of a different aesthetic: young, beautiful, pure from
all the gross or obscene elements which are an integral part
of the figure of the Dagda. He is as different from the
Dagda as a classical Apollo from a primitive idol. His
weapon is not the club but the spear, the Irish casting-spear
which was a sort of javelin. And he also uses the sling,
for it was with a sling-stone that he killed Balor of the
poisonous eye, chief of the Fomorians. He is called Lám-
fhada ('Lug of the Long Arm'), and the epithet refers not
to his solar nature, as has been supposed, although there is
nothing in the mythology to confirm it, but to his manner
of warfare. Lug can wound from a distance by means of
his casting weapons, and in this respect he differs from the
Dagda, who wields the ancient club, as the young repre-

[1] cf. A. H. Krappe, 'Les Dieux au Corbeau chez les Celtes', *Revue de l'histoire des religions*, 114, 236.

sentative of technical progress differs from an old chieftain with antique weapons, witness of an outmoded culture.

Another of Lug's titles confirms this quality. He is called the *Samildánach*, literally 'he who possesses at the same time (*sam-*) many (*il*) skills (*dán*)', the many-skilled. A story tells[1] 'that when he presented himself at the assembly of the *Tuatha*, the porter asked him before admitting him: 'What skill have you, for no one is admitted to Tara unless he have some skill?' 'I am a carpenter,' said Lug. 'We do not need you,' is the answer, 'for we have a carpenter.' 'I am a smith,' said Lug. But the *Tuatha* have a smith. Lug then insists that he is also harper, poet, historian, champion, hero and sorcerer. The *Tuatha* have among them specialists in all these crafts, but they have no one who combines them all. And so they receive Lug into their company.

We see that the title *Samildánach* does not characterize Lug as a god of crafts, a sort of Celtic Mercury, in contrast with gods of war or magic; for magic and warfare are among the gifts of which he boasts in this passage. And in what follows we find him taking the part of a warrior when he kills Balor in single combat, and of a magician when, before rushing into the battle, he goes around the army 'on one foot and with one eye', singing an incantation, the old trick of magic that was used in the first battle of Ireland (s. p. 5.).

Lug and the Dagda are thus opposed, not as having different functions (both can perform every function, being masters of all knowledge), but inasmuch as they represent different and certainly successive conceptions of that knowledge from which man expects the mastery of the world, and which he regards as the first attribute of his gods and the source of their power. These two conceptions find expression in the two titles of the gods: the Dagda is the

[1] RC 12, 75. § 55.

Ruad Ro-fhessa, the 'Lord of Great Knowledge', knowledge one and undifferentiated; the young Lug is the *Samildánach*, possessed of many skills, expert in the various specialities into which the unity of primitive culture is separated with the advance of technical ingenuity. The Dagda maintains the prestige which attaches to ancient things. Lug enjoys the popularity belonging to new fashions. Thus the heroic sagas have adopted Lug and made him the father of Cú Chulainn, but not the Dagda, who had no place in a world dominated by new conceptions and a new aesthetic.

The other gods of the *Tuatha*, king Nuada, the champion Ogma, and the local chieftains, each of whom reigns over a separate domain and commands his own troops, as, for example, Midir of Brí Léith in County Longford, or Bodb of Síd ar Femen in Tipperary, all these represent merely variants, more or less individualized, of the type of the Chieftain-God. But we must distinguish one class of gods, who, though reckoned among the chiefs of the *Tuatha Dé Danann*, are akin in some respects to the class of mother-goddesses. These are the sea-gods, among whom the most prominent is Manannán Son of Ler, one of the most poetic figures of Celtic mythology.

Manannán mac Lir takes his name from the Isle of Man (Irish *Inis Manann*). He appears also in Welsh mythology as Manawyddan ab Llyr. His original domain extends therefore across the Irish Sea. Poets describe him travelling over the sea in his chariot; and the chariot is the ordinary vehicle of the goddesses, from *Morrígan* to Flidais, but not of the other male gods. For him the sea is a plain sown with purple flowers, and the speckled salmon are leaping lambs. Thus he appears to the navigator who voyages in search of The Land of Youth (*Tír na nÓc*) and of the Isles of the Blessed. One tradition, which preserves a memory of the multiple nature of the god, distinguishes four Manannáns.[1]

[1] Thurneysen, *Heldensage*, 516.

The faculty of assuming animal form is attributed, not indeed to the god himself, but to his son Mongán:

'He will be in the shape of every beast,
Both on the azure sea and on land,
He will be a dragon before hosts . . .
He will be a wolf of every great forest.

He will be a stag with horns of silver
In the land where chariots are driven,
He will be a speckled salmon in a full pool,
He will be a seal, he will be a fair white swan.'[1]

Behind Manannán, and as it were, eclipsed by him, we can perceive other, more ancient sea-gods: Ler, father of Manannán, who is for us only a name; the Fomorian Tethra, of whom it is said that fish are his 'cattle', just as the beasts of the forest are the 'cattle' of Flidais; Nechtán, if, as is probable, his name is etymologically cognate with that of Neptune.[2] A name or a petrified formula are all that survive of these forgotten gods. If the gods of the sea have certain traits in common with the goddesses of the earth, the chariot in which they travel, a multiple form, the association with animal species, they differ from them, it seems, in one respect. While the goddesses survive, the sea-gods succeed each other. It would appear that each new group of invaders brought their own sea-god and annexed for him the newly conquered seas, but that they adopted the local goddesses who were attached to the soil, an immovable legacy from their predecessors.

[1] Kuno Meyer, *Imram Brain*, i, 24.
[2] Hubert, in Czarnowski, *Le Culte des héros*, p. xix, n. 1.

CHAPTER V

THE FEAST OF THE FIRST OF NOVEMBER

THE day on which the race of men triumphed over the race of gods marks the end of the mythical period when the supernatural was undisputed master of the earth, and the beginning of a new period in which men and gods inhabit the earth together. From that moment the great problem of religion becomes important, the problem of the relationship between man and the gods. The mythology states the circumstances in which the charter regulating this relationship was established once and for all.[1]

The power of the vanquished gods was still considerable. Since they controlled the fertility of the soil, they could reduce men to submission by denying them its fruits. Thus they deprived the Sons of Míl of harvests and of milk, and so compelled their king to treat with them. It was agreed to divide the country into two equal parts. The poet Amairgin made the division: the *Tuatha Dé Danann* received the lower half of Ireland, the territory under the earth, and the Sons of Míl the upper half, the surface of the earth. It was thus that the gods, retiring under ground, took possession of those mounds, some prehistoric *tumuli*, others natural formations, which the Irish peasant still regards as the habitations of the fairies, and which the Dagda long ago distributed among his people, appointing one *Síd* for Lug and another for Ogma. Not only mounds and caves but also deep waters belong to the gods. Beneath 'Bird Lake' in Connaught there is a *Síd*, and it is from there that king Crimthann Cas once saw the spirit Fiachna come

[1] Thurneysen, *Heldensage*, 604 and 474.

47

forth to ask for help against a hostile chieftain-god. He
led the king and his warriors back into his domain under
the lake.[1]   The sea covers one province of this hidden
world, *Tír fo Thuinn* ('The Land under the Waves').
Even the islands perceived or imagined out in the ocean,
all those *terrae incognitae* over which Manannán and Tethra
hold sway, belong to the share of the divine race with
which man has divided the world. Not only the recesses
of the earth, regions under ground or beneath the ocean,
but also the mysterious frontiers of the world controlled
by the Sons of Míl, all that lies outside the narrow circle
that is lit by the bright and comfortable light of the fires
of men, belongs to those invisible and powerful neighbours,
the people of the *Síd, áes síde*. So too for the primitive the
supernatural world begins with the wilderness, almost at the
gates of his village.

The poets delight in describing this hidden world, often
in the gayest colours and in terms of highest praise. In
this Land of Youth (*Tír na nÓc*), this Delightful Plain (*Mag
Mell*) rich in fruits and flowers, men and women, eternally
young and divinely beautiful, dwell in palaces sparkling
with precious stones and metals, intoxicated with mead
from an inexhaustible vat, lulled by the music of many
birds or by the melody of an apple-branch with flowers
of crystal whose sound soothes grief and brings peaceful
slumber. This idyllic life has however its episodes of warfare. For those peaceful pleasures, love, intoxication, music,
chariot-races, are not enough without the favourite pastime
of the Celt, which was war. Causes of battle were not
lacking between the chieftains of neighbouring *Síde*, and
sometimes one of the parties seeks the aid of a human king
or hero, offering him in payment for his services the love
of a fairy mistress.

Other stories describe this supernatural world in less

[1] S. H. O'Grady, *Silva Gadelica*, ii, 290.

favourable terms. There are fortresses guarded by monsters, into which the hero must force his way to do battle, sword in hand, with hostile deities. One such is the kingdom of Shadow (*Scáth*) where Cú Chulainn makes a raid (s. p. 74). The question arises whether we should regard these two types of myth as representing opposite conceptions of the supernatural world, one gay and the other horrible. Should we distinguish two supernatural regions and identify the happy Land of Youth as a Celtic Olympus or Valhalla, where the gods dwell, and the gloomy region of *Scáth* as a Hades or Erebus, kingdom of the dead? There is nothing in the native tradition which authorizes us to suppose this dualism. There is no irresolvable conflict between the two types of story, and the transition from one to the other is quite easy. The violence which prevails in the kingdom of *Scáth* is not unknown in the blessed *Síd*, and there too man sometimes arrives by force in search of plunder. The myths of *Samain* discussed below are evidence of this. These different abodes are inhabited by the same race, a race which is not the race of men living or dead. If it is described in various lights, sometimes favourable and sometimes forbidding, it is because the relations which it maintains with men are various. In the stories in which the hero is invited as an ally by the folk of the *Síd* the poet delights in describing the magnificence of the welcome he receives and of the abode he visits. But if it is an account of the exploit of one who is not afraid to make war upon superhuman adversaries, the blackest colours are used to paint the dangers which he encounters and the terrors which he overcomes. Thus the same people appear in a quite different light, according as they are approached as hosts or as enemies.

These folk of the *Síd* who lead a life so like that of men, an ideal reflection of the life of the warlike Celtic aristocracy, do not differ much from men except in one respect.

Being eternally young, they are, we are told, immortal. This at least is what Caílte, the Ossianic hero, says of one of them: 'I am mortal, for I am of the race of men, but she is immortal, for she is of the race of the *Tuatha Dê Danann*.' Nevertheless we have accounts of the death of one or another of the people of the *Tuatha*, and we know that they can even be killed by men. Thus Finn slew with his spear the spirit whose fiery breath set Tara in flames. And this is not merely part of the incoherence that Celtic mythology allows. The apparent contradiction is resolved, when we consider the notion of immortality in the light of what may be called the intemporal character of the *Síd*.

The people of the *Síd* may be mortal by accident, liable to wounds, and subject to a violent death which, for the primitive, is the most natural sort of death. They are none the less immortal in essence, inasmuch as they know nothing of old age and time has no hold upon them; for they live in a world which is not subject to time. It is a constant law of the supernatural world that whoever enters there escapes from human time. When Bran and his comrades, having dwelt in the Isles of the Blessed, are seized with nostalgia and want to see again the shores of their native country, their hosts are careful to warn them that they must refrain from setting foot on land. When they have come within calling distance of the shore, they question the Irishmen who have gathered there, asking whether they remember Bran mac Febail. 'We know no one of that name,' they say, 'but our old stories tell of Bran.' One of Bran's companions cannot resist the attraction of his native soil, but hardly has he touched it when he falls in ashes to the ground.[1] This passage has been interpreted as evidence that the Islands are a land of the dead, and Bran and his companions ghosts. But these navigators came alive into the Islands, and alive they dwelt

[1] Kuno Meyer, *Imram Brain*, i, 32.

there for centuries, which seemed to them as short as years. The moment that one of them abandons that world beyond time, the centuries passed fall upon him at once, and re-entering the world of human time, he dies.

Nera, on his return from the *Síd*, has a similar experience, but in reverse. When he rejoins his companions, having passed three days in the *Síd*, he finds them around the camp-fire by which he had left them, before dishes which have not had time to cook during his absence. Just as our measure of time is foreign to the *Síd*, so also is our measure of space. A mound of modest dimensions contains a whole people with their dwellings and lands. Although in close prox-imity, the two worlds, situated on different planes, are not subject to the same dimensions.

The two races, one imperishable if not immortal, and the other subject to decay, are nevertheless regarded as equal in rights and dignity: 'There are only two races of equal (*cudruma*) rights in Ireland, the Sons of Míl and the *Tuatha*.' They maintain neighbourly relations with each other whether friendly or hostile. They receive each other's exiles, as is the practice between human clans. When the three sons of the king of Ireland are refused a portion by their father, they visit the *Tuatha* and fast against them, according to the Celtic procedure of the hunger-strike— which goes back to Indo-European tradition, for we find it in India. The *Tuatha*, yielding to this pressure, give them wives and fortunes in the *Síd*, and they remain there.[1] Conversely, Finn takes into service in his warrior-band (s. p. 82) a deserter from the *Síd*, who is dissatisfied with the lot appointed to him by his people.

The two worlds are thus in frequent contact and exchanges are possible, but they are none the less distinct and mutually almost impervious, each race respecting the established *modus vivendi* and abstaining from trespass upon the domain

[1] S. H. O'Grady, *Silva Gadelica*, ii, 110.

of the other. However, there is a time when the invisible
magic partition which separates them is withdrawn, and
the two worlds are in free communication, the two planes
become one, as was the case in the mythical period. This
happens during the night of *Samain* (from the thirty-first
of October to the first of November), the eve of the Celtic
New Year. This night belongs neither to one year nor the
other, and is, as it were, free from temporal restraint. It
seems that the whole supernatural force is attracted by the
seam thus left at the point where the two years join, and
gathers to invade the world of men.

The feast of *Samain* is one of the four great feasts of the
Celtic year, one of the four periods at which peoples,
normally dispersed over territories that had no great centres
of population, came together for a social and religious
purpose, and were assembled for some days in a sacred
place, a sort of temporary sanctuary, to celebrate the feast.
Samain (the first of November), 'the Pagan Easter', and
Cétshamain, or *Beltine* (the first of May) divide the year into
two seasons, the cold season (Gaulish *Giamon-*, Irish *gem-
red*, Welsh *gaiaf*), and the hot season (Gaulish *Samon-*,
Irish *sam-rad*, Welsh *haf*). This division is common to the
whole Celtic world, for we find traces of it in the Coligny
Calendar and in modern Welsh usage (*Calan gaiaf, Calan
Mai*).[1] Each season is divided, at least in Ireland, into two
halves by the feasts of *Imbolc* (the First of February), now
the feast of St. Brigid, and *Lugnasad* (the First of August).
We see that the Celtic calendar is regulated not by the
solar year, by solstice and equinox, but by the agrarian and
pastoral year, by the beginning and end of the tasks of
cattle-raising and agriculture. So, too, Celtic mythology
is dominated by goddesses of the earth, and one looks in
vain for solar deities. These two connected facts betray the
same orientation of religious thought.

[1] J. Loth, RC 25, 125.

The feast of *Lugnasad*, placed under the protection of various mother-goddesses (s. p. 26), that of *Imbolc*, St. Brigid's Day, on which, according to Cormac the Glossator, the lactation of ewes begins, and *Beltine* which gets its name from the great fires between which the cattle were driven to protect them against sickness, have a marked agrarian character. And this character is not alien to *Samain*—for every feast tends to be a total celebration—but it is driven into the background by other characteristics which give to this feast its sombre and fanciful atmosphere. *Samain* is not the feast of any one tutelary deity, but rather of the whole world of spirits, whose intrusion upon the world of men takes on a threatening and warlike air.

Samain is the time when the tithes levied upon the harvest of the fruitful season are offered, in this barren season, to the spirits. These sacrifices take on the character not of offerings to guardian powers but of a heavy tribute imposed on man by the powers of destruction. Thus the race of Nemed is forced to deliver to the Fomorians 'two-thirds of their milk, their corn and their children'. So, too, until the coming of Saint Patrick, according to the *Dindshenchas*, the Irish used to offer on the first of November to Crom Cruaich, or Cenn Cruaich ('the Curve of the Mound' or 'the Chief of the Mound') 'the firstlings of every issue and the chief scions of every clan'. The king of Ireland, Tigernmas, and the men and women of Ireland used to prostrate themselves before him 'so that the tops of their foreheads and the gristle of their noses and the caps of their knees and the ends of their elbows broke, and three-fourths of the men of Ireland perished at those prostrations'.[1] The description is fantastic, but it evokes the memory of a bloody rite based upon terror.

There is a whole cycle of myths about the time of *Samain*. They tell of meetings, usually hostile, between two worlds.

[1] *The Rennes Dindshenchas* § 85 (RC 16, 35).

The Battle of Mag Tured is essentially a myth of *Samain*. The legend of Muirchertach mac Erca, who was attacked by the people of the *Síd* and perished, half-drowned in a vat and half-scorched in the burning of his house (a double death which recalls sacrificial rites), is a myth of *Samain*.[1] The strange story of the *Intoxication of the Ulstermen*,[2] which tells the wild escapade of the heroes wandering through Ireland confused by darkness and intoxication, and escaping only with difficulty from death 'in a white-hot house', evidently of sacrificial character, is a myth of orgic frenzy proper to this night of confusion.

Among these stories there is an episode of the *Adventure of Nera*,[3] which illustrates the relations between men and the folk of the *Síd* at this exceptional time. Nera, a warrior of Ailill, king of Connacht, set out into the forest on a fanciful adventure which we may here neglect. On his way home he finds the king's house at Ráith Cruachain in flames, while a hostile army is engaged in collecting the heads they have taken. He follows the army and enters the Cavern of Cruachu, a cave from which fantastic animals are sometimes seen to emerge, and one of the *Síde* of Ireland. He becomes the husband of a woman of the *Síd*. She tells him that the burning of Ráith Cruachain is an illusion, but that it will become reality if the *Síd* is not destroyed the next *Samain* night. Nera returns to his companions, whom he finds seated peacefully around their fire. The warriors must only wait till the next *Samain* night, the night 'when all the *Síde* of Ireland are open', to make their attack. When the fated time comes, they attack and plunder the *Síd*, and carry off their booty. Nera alone remains in the *Síd*, and he will live there with his wife until the Day of Judgement.

---

[1] S. Czarnowski, *Le culte des héros*, 120.
[2] Thurneysen, *Heldensage*, 473.
[3] *op. cit.*, 311.

The burning of Ráith Cruachain is only an illusion, but this is not true of the burning of Tara, which is the subject of another myth.[1] Every *Samain* night Aillén mac Midhna, one of the *Tuatha Dé Danann*, comes forth from his *Síd* and vomits against Tara a stream of fire which sets it on fire. This is repeated for twenty-three years, until Finn, having reached the age of ten and taken his place in the assembly of Tara, kills Aillén. This exploit won him the command of the *Fiana*, the warrior-bands of Ireland (s. chap. VII).

The theme of all these myths is the same: an attack by the troops of the other world upon the dwellings of men, sometimes followed by a successful counter-attack. The motifs of fire and of water, sometimes associated, appear in various forms, dwellings set on fire, an iron house made white-hot, or drowning in a vat, which resemble certain methods of human sacrifice attested for the Celts of the continent. We know from the scholiast of Lucan[2] that Teutates was propitiated by the drowning of victims in a vat, and Taranis by burning them in a wooden vessel. These savage rites are in accord with the religious atmosphere of a time when the supernatural was a wanton power and assumed a very menacing character.

There are, however, other myths of *Samain* in which the two orders appear in a different light, for example, the legend of *The Wasting Sickness of Cú Chulainn* which tells of the hero's visit to the *Síd* where he enjoys the love of the fairy Fann.[3] In this myth, the motif of warfare, while not quite absent, is secondary to the sexual motif. In this respect the episode of the Dagda's meeting with the *Morrígan* is comparable. What is characteristic of the time is not the manner of the meeting of the two worlds, but

[1] S. H. O'Grady, *Silva Gadelica*, ii, 142.
[2] *Commenta Bernensia*, ed. Usener, 32.
[3] Thurneysen, *Heldensage*, 413.

the fact that they meet. During this night of chaos, the conditions of the mythical period are renewed and a world normally closed to men is opened, just as at Rome, on the ritual days when the stone which closes the entrance to the subterranean region is raised, *mundus patet*.[1]

The Church, careful to annex earlier traditions that were difficult to uproot, has made this feast of all the spirits into the feast of all the saints, our All Saints' Day. The Christian conception has obliterated the specific character of the Celtic conception, a reciprocal relationship between the visible and invisible worlds, which permitted men, when the spirits invaded their world, to attack in their turn those mysterious dwellings which for one night lay open and accessible.

[1] cf. R. Caillois, *L'homme et le sacré*, 108.

CHAPTER VI

THE HERO OF THE TRIBE

THE world of the Celts appears to be populated with supernatural beings who are co-proprietors of the soil. Man has won his domain from them either by force or by the subtle violence of magic; and with them he maintains a relationship of rival powers, friendly and hostile alternately. In contrast to these beings conceived in his image, but strangers to his race, the Celt composed a mythical figure which is purely human, magnified indeed to the extreme limit of humanity, but not beyond. This is the hero, the incarnation of the ideal qualities of the race.

There may be analogies between god and hero; but there is no transition. The opposition between the two is not formal and does not depend on particular characteristics: it is functional, depending on the part played by the hero on the one hand and the god on the other in this mythical world which is divided into two camps. The hero is in the camp of men. Gods, spirits, elves, fairies, however one imagines them, whatever name one gives them, are in the other camp. The hero is of our race, the race of the Sons of Míl. He is one of us. The others, even though they be protectors or allies, are of another race, that of the *Tuatha Dé Danann*, or of some other prehistoric race, in any case utter strangers.

Celtic languages have many names for the hero. The commonest name in the Irish texts, which were compiled by Christian monks, is a Latin loanword, *láech*, from the Latin *laicus*, and means the 'layman' who bears arms, in opposition to the cleric who is exempt. This term has replaced, in the correct usage of a Christian society, ancient

Celtic words which express a quite different conception:
nia, lath gaile, cur (caur), arg, donn.

Nia can be explained as from a stem *neit- which belongs
to the root from which the name of *Mars Neto* is derived
and which recurs in Irish *níth* 'combat', Welsh *nwyd* 'ardour,
passion'. Germanic has a series of similar words for the
notions of warlike ardour, hostility and hatred. Another
extension of the same root provides Irish *niab* 'vivacity,
energy', Welsh *nwyf* 'excitement', and, no doubt, also Irish
nóeb 'holy', holiness being originally imagined as an active
force. The hero is thus here conceived as the ardent one,
as one who overflows with energy and life.[1]

An analogous conception finds expression in *lath gaile*.
The second term *gal* 'valour' doubtless belongs to the root
of Anglo-Saxon *glēd* 'flame'. It would then really mean
'ardour'. The etymology of *lath* is obscure, but the word
is not to be separated from the homonym *lath* 'rut', a
meaning which sometimes attaches to Welsh *nwyf* cited
above. Here we have two specializations, one sexual, the
other military, of a single notion of ardour or excitement,
which we noted in Irish *nia*.

Cur or *caur* (cognate with Gaulish καυαρος) is connected
with a root which means 'to swell' (cf. Sanskrit *śavas*
'strength, power'). The episode in the *Cattle-Raid of
Cualnge*, in which Cú Chulainn, in the fury of combat,
'inflates himself and swells like a bladder full of air,'[2] explains the connection that is possible between the notions
of 'swelling' and of military strength or ardour.

Other terms used occasionally by the poets are *arg*,
cognate with Greek ἀργος 'swift', or *donn*, corresponding to
Gaulish *dusius*, perhaps cognate with Greek θῦα 'bacchant'.
Irish *dásacht* 'warlike fury' may belong to the same root.

We see that all the words for 'hero' express the notions

[1] Vendryes, RC 46, 265.
[2] Windisch, *Táin Bó Cúalnge*, 3802.

of fury, ardour, tumescence, speed. The hero is the furious one, possessed of his own tumultuous and blazing energy.

This heroic fury is personified especially in Sétanta-Cú Chulainn, around whom Irish heroic mythology has crystallized itself. His first name, which he received at birth, is Sétanta. This name cannot be separated from that of the Setantii whom Ptolemy places on the west coast of Britain opposite to the hero's domain, Mag Muirthemne, across the Irish Sea.[1] Cú Chulainn was thus originally the eponymous hero of a tribe belonging to the British family of Celts. Yet he is not an ancestor. While other lesser heroes, such as Conall Cernach, are ancestors of numerous clans, the hero *par excellence* will die without leaving any posterity. The prestige which surrounds him owes nothing to the veneration in which people hold the great dead from whom they claim descent. His relationship to his people is a different one: he is their defender and their champion. He is the ideal type of youth, of fighter, at once the glory and the living rampart of his tribe. Sometimes he is called Sétanta son of Dechtire, his mother's name; and this form preserves the memory of matriarchal conceptions of which we have already seen traces elsewhere (s. p. 37.).

Two versions of the story of his supernatural birth are extant[2]. The earlier of the two will be summarized here.

The fields around Emain Macha had been devastated by a flock of birds which devoured to the roots everything that grew there. With some misgiving, for they suspect the presence of some mysterious power, the people of Ulster harness nine chariots to hunt the birds. They are led by king Conchobor, whose charioteer is his daughter, or, as some say, his sister Dechtire. They follow the birds which are in nine flocks, with twenty in every flock, tied in pairs with chains of gold, and singing sweetly. Night overtakes the hunters near Brug na Bóinne, the most famous fairy

[1] Ptolemy 2, 3, 3.
[2] Thurneysen, *Heldensage*, 268.

dwelling in Ireland and the home of the Dagda. The chariots are unharnessed, and two warriors go in search of a lodging. They come to a little house inhabited by a man and a woman. In their necessity, they bring the whole company there, and by some miracle the house proves big enough to shelter them all, and the food enough to satisfy and intoxicate them. During the night the woman gives birth to a son. At the same time a mare foals twin foals which are bestowed upon the newly born child. These will become the two famous horses of the hero, The Grey of Macha and the Black of Saingliu.

According to the second version, the woman was Dechtire herself, who had mysteriously disappeared with fifty of her companions, and whom the Ulstermen had sought in vain for three years. According to the first version, the child is simply given into the care of Dechtire.

In the morning, the house and its hosts have disappeared. Only the two foals and the infant remain. The infant dies. Dechtire is in despair, and the warriors chant the funeral lament. The hero seems to have died at birth but he will be re-born. In a dream, Dechtire sees a strange man approach her. He reveals that he is the god Lug. It is he who has brought her into the *Síd*. She will bear a son who will be the son of Lug—or rather, according to another tradition, presenting a different conception, this child is Lug himself: thus this divine birth is a reincarnation. Dechtire becomes pregnant. The Ulstermen, unable to understand this mystery, accuse Conchobor of begetting a child in drunkenness upon his own sister who slept beside him, in the promiscuity of the primitive Celtic home.[1] In this way there appears in the myth, beside the motif of divine origin, the motif of incestuous origin, which was also sacred and is of frequent occurrence in the heroic sagas.

[1] Brother and sister sleep together in certain communities in the Caucasus, Claude Lévi-Strauss, *Word*, i, 45 [Tr.].

Conchobor betroths his sister to the warrior Sualtaim. But Dechtire, ashamed to marry in her condition, causes an abortion. She becomes pregnant again, and this time the child is born and lives. Tradition says that this child is the same that was born once before and that was about to be born a second time, so that Sétanta is called the 'son of three years' because he 'was born three times'. We see that the triple form which characterizes so many Celtic divinities recurs in the person of the hero, not simultaneous here, but successive, and thus compatible with the unity of a human being.

First a name is chosen for the child, Sétanta. Then he must have fosterparents, for the Celtic infant was not reared by his own parents, but was entrusted to other members of the clan. The bond created by this fosterage was regarded as more sacred than the natural bond. While other children have only one fosterfather and one foster-mother, the education of the future hero requires the collaboration of the most eminent representatives of the tribe, as though he belonged from that moment to the whole community: the poet Amairgin rears him, but the Irish Nestor, Sencha, teaches him wisdom, the hero Fergus teaches him the use of weapons, the druid Cathbad teaches him the arts of the gods of magic.

He grows to the age of seven years without record. Then, taking his wooden weapons, childish toys, he sets out to join the hundred and fifty boys who are reared at the king's palace. Here begins the series of initiation feats from which he emerges triumphant to take his place among grown men.[1]

From the moment of his entrance into the company of his equals in age, he displays that insolent excess, that ὕβϵις which Greek wisdom condemns as a defiance of fate, but which the Celts seem to have regarded as the great

[1] Thurneysen, *op. cit.*, 130.

virtue of a hero.   Having refused the protection of his
elders he is attacked by all the hundred and fifty boys who
throw at him their hundred and fifty hurley sticks.   He
wards them off so cleverly that not one of them strikes
him (a feat that we shall observe again, p. 83, in the initiation
of a candidate for the *fiana*).   Then for the first time there
comes over him the terrible contortion which is the manifestation of his warlike valour.   He revolves in his skin
so that his feet and knees are behind, and his calves and
buttocks in front.   His hair stands on end, and on the tip
of each hair there is a drop of blood, or, in other versions,
a spark of fire.   His mouth, wide open so that his gullet
is seen, emits a stream of fire.   One of his eyes recedes
into his skull so far that a heron could not pick it out.
The other, as big as a cauldron, protrudes on to his cheek.
A strange emanation called the 'hero's moon' rises from
his forehead 'as thick as a whet-stone'.   From his skull
rises a stream of black blood as high as the mast of a
ship.

These contortions have a parallel in Celtic tradition
and also in Scandinavian.   The huge eye in the middle of
the cheek, the streams flowing from the skull and the mouth,
the strange sign on the forehead, are features that we find
on the head of Ogmios upon the coins of Armorica.[1]
These are therefore images common to the insular Celts and
to their cousins on the continent.   And the sign 'as thick
as a whetstone' has been compared to the whetstone fixed
in the head of Thorr, the grimace of Sétanta to that of the
viking Egill when he 'lowered one eyebrow to his chin
and raised the other to the roots of his hair'.[2]   In both
cases we have to do with a sort of stigmata, signs of the
initiation in warfare which the hero's first exploit confers,
and at the same time manifestations of the fury which

[1] Sjoestedt-Jonval, *Etudes Celtiques*, i, 8.
[2] Dumézil, *Mythes et Dieux des Germains*, 105.

characterizes the fierce *berserkir* of Scandinavia as well as the Irish heroes.[1]

Sétanta pursues his adversaries in triumph to where the king sits, and leaps over the king's chessboard. He leaves them scattered on the ground, and their fosterparents come to pick them up. Then he presents himself to his uncle, and requires that the other boys shall be under his protection in future, and not he under theirs as is the custom.

This entrance of the hero into the social circle, entrance by force as it might be called, recalls, in spite of the difference of circumstances, the *début* of a certain Welsh hero. When the young Kulhwch comes to present himself to his uncle, King Arthur,[2] the porter, in conformity with the rule of the court, refuses to admit him, because the banquet has begun, but offers him meanwhile abundant hospitality. The youth replies to this courteous offer by threatening, if he is not admitted at once, to utter three mortal shouts (the shout known as 'louder than the abyss' was a legal form of protest) such that all the pregnant women on the island will abort and the others will suffer such agony that their wombs will turn within them and they will never conceive. When his request is granted, he enters on horseback although all the other heroes used to dismount at the gate. It seems to be the rule for a great hero to enter always by violence, even into his own social group, and that, before becoming a member of society, he must establish himself against it in disregard of its customs and even of the royal authority.

Having taken his place at the head of the boys of his age, Sétanta has to face a series of ordeals. First there are phantoms and their terrors. One evening on the field of battle, where he has gone in search of the king who has been wounded, he meets 'a man with half a head bearing on his shoulders half a man'. The man asks him to relieve him of his burden, and, on his refusal, throws it on to his shoulders. They fight and the child is thrown down. Then the voice of the *Badb* is heard from the corpses. 'Here is a poor apprentice-hero', said she, 'trampled under foot by a phantom.' Sétanta gets up then, cuts off the monster's head with his hurley stick (for he has no other weapon), and goes off driving the head like a ball before him across the battle-field.

After the phantom comes a ferocious beast, the famous hound of Culann, the smith, who alone protected all the herds of his master, and whom it took nine men to hold in leash. One evening when the Ulstermen were feasting at the house of Culann, and the dog had been turned loose for the night, Sétanta, who had been forgotten, arrived and found himself face to face with the beast. The Ulstermen did not dare to go out, for fear that they would be torn to pieces. But the child hurled his ball into the brute's throat so that he tore out its entrails. All rejoiced. Only Culann lamented his loss. Then Sétanta undertook to protect Culann and his herds and the whole plain of Muirthemne in place of the dog, so that none should take a beast without his knowledge. 'You will be called henceforth "The Hound of Culann" (*Cú Chulainn*),' said the Ulstermen. Thus Sétanta received his definitive name, his name as a man, at the moment when he solemnly assumed the function, which was to be his, of protector of the land and property of his people.

He now needs only a warrior's equipment, and the druid who knows the auspicious and inauspicious days must appoint the time. Once when Cathbad was instructing his hundred pupils, one of them questioned him about the virtue of that day. Cathbad replied that he who should take arms on that day would be famous for ever throughout Ireland for his exploits. Cú Chulainn overheard this, and went to Conchobor to ask for arms, pretending to have been sent by Cathbad. The king sent for arms, but the child broke fifteen sets of weapons until the weapons of the king himself were brought. Then Cathbad arrived and explained the ruse, adding that he who should take arms that day would die young. But Cú Chulainn preferred a short life followed by lasting fame to a long life without glory. He repeated the ruse to obtain a chariot, the chariot of the king himself. Then he set out, in celebration of his taking of arms, for his first excursion beyond the limits of the province. On the way he met Conall Cernach, older than he, who was on duty at the frontier to offer a welcome to every poet and combat to every warrior who should present himself. Cú Chulainn offered to relieve him, thus announcing that he considered himself fit to perform this duty of guardian of the territory which seems to be the function of the Celtic hero. Repulsed by Conall, who thought him fit to receive a poet, but not a warrior, he went on his way and penetrated into strange, that is to say enemy, country. He defied in single combat the three sons of Nechta Scéne, who had killed more Ulstermen than were left alive, cut off their heads, and returned to Emain Macha. On the way he brought down a flock of swans without killing them, with two shots from his sling, and tied them with the reins of his chariot. Then he captured a deer, subduing it with a mere glance, and thus proved his magical ascendancy over animals as well as his skill as a hunter. He arrived in view of Emain, in magnificent style, 'the deer trotting behind, the swans flying overhead, and the three heads in the chariot'.

But the sentry at watch on the walls of Emain was alarmed to see him returning still a prey to the violent ecstasy which did not distinguish friend from enemy. And indeed the chariot, as it came before the rampart, presented the left side, in violation of a tabu (*geis*). This was another

deliberate infraction of the consecrated order. 'I swear by
the god by whom the men of Ulster swear,' cried Cú
Chulainn, 'that if there is no man to give me combat, I
will shed the blood of all those in the fort!' 'Let naked
women go to meet him!' said the king. And Mugain,
the queen, and her women did so. While he was thus
confused (the Christian redactors interpret this as a sign of
modesty[1]), he was seized and plunged successively into
three vats of cold water. The first burst asunder, the second
boiled in great bubbles, the third became warm. Having
been calmed by this means, he could be re-admitted to the
household without danger.

How should we understand the intervention of the
women in this episode? Should we take it, with the
redactor, as a means of causing the transgressor to be
ashamed of his absurd misbehaviour? ('These are the men
that you will have to fight,' said the queen.) Or as an
expedient analogous to that which Caesar attributes to the
women of Gergovia for the purpose of turning the fierce-
ness of a warrior towards thoughts less bloody?[2] Or again
as recourse to the magic of sacred nakedness[3] as a pro-
pitiatory rite? We know that the women of Britain appeared naked in certain religious ceremonies.[4] This episode,
coming at the end of a series of initiatory ordeals, becomes
clear if we compare it with scenes of a sexual character which
accompany the tribal initiation of young men in various
primitive communities.[5] The young man enters into the
class of men, to whom commerce with the women of the
tribe is permitted. He has sexually come of age.[6]

The queen then dresses him in a tunic and a blue cloak

---

[1] See preface, p. v [Tr.].
[2] *De Bello Gallico*, vii, 47.
[3] Vendryes, RC 45, 157.
[4] Pliny, *Natural History*, xxii, 2.
[5] There is a résumé of the question of tribal initiation in H. Jeanmaire, *Couroi et Courètes*, 172.
[6] This interpretation has been suggested to me by G. Dumézil.

held by a silver brooch—his manly garments, his *toga virilis*. Then he takes the place at the king's knee which he shall occupy henceforth. Let us pause to consider the personality of the candidate at the moment when he has been accepted as a hero.

He is beautiful, of a beauty rather baroque than classic, which corresponds in some points to the ideal suggested by the figurines on Gaulish coins, and the descriptions given by ancient historians of the continental Celts.[1] His hair, of three colours, 'brown on the crown of his head, red in the middle and fringed with gold, forms a triple braid before it falls in ringlets on his shoulders. A hundred strings of jewels decorate his head, a hundred collars of gold glitter on his breast. His cheeks are flushed with four colours, yellow, blue, green and red. Seven pupils shine in each eye, his hands have seven fingers, his feet seven toes. Thus the sacred number is inscribed all over his person. Holding nine captured heads in one hand and ten in the other, he juggles with them, parading happily before the people and offering himself to the admiration of poets, craftsmen and women.

Such is, at least, his normal appearance, when he is not a prey to those contortions, which have earned him the title of contortionist and which resemble those of the *shamans*. Another title of the hero expresses the truly demoniac side of his nature: he is called the *síabartha*, a term often applied to elves and phantoms, and formed from a root expressing the notions of illusion, magic prestige and sorcery.[2] Thus the personality of the hero combines the features of warrior and magician.

This personality is further defined by a certain number of excellences and accomplishments, *buada* and *clessa*, as well as a series of personal tabus (*geasa*). Every Irish hero

---

[1] Sjoestedt-Jonval, *Etudes Celtiques*, i, 21.
[2] Vendryes, RC 46, 263.

has his 'excellences' (*buada*), as every Welsh hero has his 'faculties' (*cynneddfau*), by which he is distinguished from ordinary mortals. Thus among the heroes of Arthur's court, Kei can breathe under water for nine days and nights; he can go without sleep for the same period; he can become as big as the biggest tree in the forest; his natural heat is so great that his comrades use it for fire; finally, no doctor can cure a wound inflicted by him.[1]

Some of these faculties are possessed likewise by Cú Chulainn. We have seen that his ardour can heat three vats of water. He can go without sleep from *Samain* until the following harvest. The wound he inflicts, even upon a goddess like the *Morrígan*, can be cured only by himself. For the rest, he possesses fifteen 'excellences' which define him as an individual accomplished in every respect: excellence in beauty, in exact judgement (he can judge to a man the number of an army from the tracks it has made), in swimming, in horsemanship, in valour (whether in line of battle or single combat), in counsel and fine language, and also in taking plunder. He knows too a number of *clessa*, those accomplishments in which warriors delight. In the house called 'Branch-Red', where the warriors of Ulster assemble around their king, we find the chariot-leaders indulging in acrobatics, crossing on a tight rope the mighty hall which is ninety-five feet long. The saga lists nineteen *clessa* of Cú Chulainn:[2] the 'salmon's leap', which is performed above the chariot in full course, the feat 'above breaths', which suggests some magic levitation ('he used to fight above the ears of the horses and the breaths of men'), stretching on a spear-head, which consists in standing on the point of a spear without hurting one's feet, the cat's leap, the wheel-turn, and a whole series of

---

[1] J. Loth, *Mabinogion,* i, 286.
[2] *Táin Bó Cúalnge*, ed. Windisch, 279.

tricks which derive from fakirism. And we may add the unfailing marksmanship which enables him to kill eight of a group of nine warriors with one cast of his javelin and leave the ninth unharmed.

Amid such a luxury of faculties, Cú Chulainn lacks the one most precious to a warrior, one which mythology readily attributes to heroes, namely invulnerability. Indeed, after the fight there is not a part of his body without a wound, and he is so shattered that the birds of the air can pass between his ribs. Celtic legend admits one invulnerable hero, like Achilles and Siegfried, namely Fer Diad Conganchness ('of skin like horn'). But the Irish rightly denied this precious faculty to their typical hero. It could only serve to diminish him in their eyes, for it offended against the ideal of Celtic heroism which involved a suicidal extreme. One is reminded of the Gauls who fought naked, as though to expose themselves more freely and then display their wounds.[1]

The superiority of the hero is not confined to the spheres of warfare and magic: it extends to what we should call intellectual culture. He is familiar with the secret, if not sacred, language called *bérla na filed* 'the jargon of the poets', a mixture of kennings, riddles like those of the Scandinavian Skalds, and traditional metaphors full of allusions to myth and ritual. When Cú Chulainn comes to woo Emer,[2] he can converse freely with her in spite of the presence of her attendants by means of this esoteric language. Thus he says that he has slept 'in the house of him who hunts the cattle of Tethra', meaning a fisherman ('the Cattle of Tethra' means 'fish'), that he has eaten 'the tabu of the chariot', meaning horseflesh, for he who has eaten horseflesh may not enter a chariot for thrice nine days. Plainly it is a language of initiates, and the initiation

[1] P. Couissin, *Annales de la Faculté des Lettres d'Aix*, xiv, 65.
[2] Thurneysen, *Heldensage*, 384.

is not restricted to men, as is the custom elsewhere, since Emer shares it with Cú Chulainn.

The personality of the hero, like that of the god, although dominantly warlike, is not specialized. To the valour of the warrior, the keen sense of the savage in the wilderness, he joins the magic skill of the sorcerer and the culture of the poet (a feature even more prominent in the Ossianic cycle where the principal heroes are poets). Every mythical idea of the Celts tends thus, in some measure, towards totality. Nevertheless this triumphant personality has a master and a limit. He finds them in the impersonal and multiform doom known as *geis*.[1]

Geis is usually translated 'tabu', and it is, indeed, like the tabu, an unconditional prohibition, a sort of categorical imperative of magical character. But it differs notably from the tabu in that the emphasis is most often placed not upon the objective passive aspect (that an object is in itself tabu), but upon the subjective active aspect (that a person is subject to a particular prohibition). Varying with the individual, it appears as an integral part of the person concerned.

There are some objective *geasa*, those which are attached to an occupation (we have just seen an example in the prohibition from eating horseflesh before entering a chariot, or entering a chariot when one has eaten horseflesh, which amounts to the same), to a place (such as the tabus of Tailtiu), or to an object, as, for instance, the tabus of the spear of Ailill Ólomm. One must not strike a stone, nor kill a woman with it, nor place it under a tooth to straighten it—this last point brings us back to the age of untempered weapons.[2] Ailill Ólomm violated all three tabus when he

---

[1] J. R. Reinhard, *The Survival of Geis in Mediaeval Romance*, and the review by Vendryes, *Etudes Celtiques*, i, 164.

[2] Cf. what Polybius says (II, 33) of the sword of the Cisalpine Gauls which bent at every stroke, so that the soldier had to straighten it against the ground with his foot.

killed Aine: the spear struck a stone after it had pierced the woman, and was bent, and he straightened it under his tooth. The poison of the spear (or rather the power of the tabu) penetrated his tooth, his breath became foul, and he became blind and insane.[1]

But most *geasa* are imagined subjectively, as inherent in the agent, not in the object. The more eminent a person is and the more sacred he is, the more *geasa* he has. The king's person is thus hedged around with prohibitions. The chief virtue of a king is to be *so-geis*, to have 'good *geasa*',[2] whatever the exact sense of the expression may be. If he is forced to infringe any one of them, he is undone. As Conaire Mór says: 'his *geasa* have seized him', and deliver him defenceless to his enemies.

Cú Chulainn could not fail to have a whole series of *geasa*.[3] Some, of a moral order, are suspect of Christian origin. Others can be explained as totemic: he may not eat the flesh of a dog, and his name is 'The Hound of Culann'. Another is a well-known form of name-tabu: he must not give his name to a single warrior. The greater part are inherent to his function of protector of the tribe: he is forbidden to allow warriors to trespass on the territory without barring their way before morning, if they come by night, or before night, if they come by day; to allow birds to feed there without bringing down some of them, or fish to come up the rivers without catching some, or even a woman to walk over the land of his people without his knowledge. In a word, he must ensure not only the defence, but the policing of the territory.

This role of defender, or watch-dog, was assumed by Cú Chulainn on the day that he received his manhood-name, and he claimed it as soon as he had taken arms,

[1] *Cóir Anmann,* § 41 (*Irische Texte,* iii, 307).
[2] Kuno Meyer, *Tecosca Cormaic,* § 6.
[3] Thurneysen, *Heldensage,* 314.

insisting upon relieving Conall who was on duty at the frontier. He fulfilled it throughout the epic which forms the centre of his cycle, the *Cattle-Raid of Cualnge*, defending the ground, alone and face to face, against the four provinces of Ireland, sleeping only for a moment at midday, 'his spear across his knees and his head on his hand'. He is responsible not only for the integrity of the territory but for the property of his people, and for their spiritual treasure of honour. Thus we have seen him encounter the fantastic equipage of the *Badb* as she drives a cow before her, and prevent the theft, for he is in charge of all the herds of Ulster. And we see him, in the *Feast of Bricriu* literally offering his head to safeguard the honour of his people, which requires that every challenge must be accepted.[1] One evening, when the heroes of Ulster are assembled in the Branch-Red House, a churl comes in. He is twice as big as the biggest of the Ulstermen, dressed in a short coarse tunic, which is the garment of the Dagda and of various mythical persons. He is Cú Roí, the local deity of Kerry. In one hand he carries an immense block, and in the other an axe. He says that he has come to seek among the heroes of the Branch-Red House what he has found nowhere else, namely one who will accord him the *fír fer*, 'truth of men', that fair play which is the warrior's code of honour, and which he cannot violate without losing face. Fergus answers that it would be a shame if none were found there to defend the honour of the province. The stranger demands that one of the heroes of Ulster (excepting only Fergus and the king) behead him, on condition that the hero allow the stranger to behead him on the morrow. It is the principle of potlatch, of total levy on condition of retribution.[2] The warrior Muinremur accepts

[1] Thurneysen, *op. cit.*, 460-61.
[2] H. Hubert, 'Le Système des prestations totales dans les littératures celtiques' RC 42, 330.

the challenge, and cuts off the churl's head. The churl picks it up, and goes off with his axe and his block. He returns the next day, but Muinremur has disappeared. Two other Ulstermen accept the ordeal in turn, but they hide when the time comes for them to honour their word. Then Cú Chulainn pledges himself. Not content with beheading the giant, he takes the precaution of cutting the head into small pieces. But the giant gets up all the same, and returns the next day. Faithful to the *fír fer*, Cú Chulainn then places his head on the block. Cú Roí raises his axe, but lets it fall so that the back of the axe strikes the blow. Then he awards to him who has thus saved the honour of his people the disputed title of first hero of Ulster. He shall be entitled in future to the 'hero's portion'[1] which consists of a cauldron in which three warriors could stand, full of pure wine. It contains a seven-year-old boar which has been fed only on milk, nuts, wheat and meat, and a seven-year-old ox which has been fed only on milk, sweet hay and corn, and a hundred wheaten cakes, cooked in honey into which have gone five and twenty bushels of flour.[2] The first exploit of Cú Chulainn, his victory over the thrice fifty boys, had won him the first place among his equals in age, the other youths. This new exploit earns him the first place among warriors.

The hero's activity is not exclusively defensive. It is offensive also. His duty is not only to protect the goods of his people, but also to enrich himself and them by profitable raids. We know that 'superiority' in pillage is one of his *buada*. Various stories tell of expeditions for plunder directed either against Scotland, or against mythical peoples or inhabitants of other worlds.[3] Thus Cú Chulainn joins with Cú Roí in leading the expedition against Echde

---

[1] A. H. Krappe, RC 48, 145.
[2] Cf. G. Henderson, *Fled Bricrend*, 9 (*Irish Texts Society*, II) [Tr.].
[3] Thurneysen, *op. cit.*, 429, 433, 569.

Horse-Mouth of Scotland, from whom the Irish carry off his three magic cows, 'the spotted ones of Echde', who fill with their milk each day the copper cauldron containing sixty pints which is called their 'calf'. Similar raids bring him against the Fir Fálgae (a mythical race more or less confused in epic tradition with the inhabitants of the Isle of Man), to Scandinavia, where he levies a tribute of seven hundred talents, and even into that province of the Other World known as the land of Shadow (*Scáth*).

The career of the hero, a résumé and model of human conduct as the Celt conceives it, would not be complete if there were no place for marriage; and we do not think that the legend of the marriage of Cú Chulainn should be considered a secondary accretion.[1] It bears the mark of the same conceptions that inspire the other sagas: it is under the seal of social conformity and ritual violence; and it includes an episode of initiatory character, comparable to those which mark the earlier stages of the hero's career.

All the women of Ulster are charmed by Cú Chulainn. To maintain order the men decide that he must have a wife of his own. The marriage is thus appointed by a common decision, in order to remove a cause of social disorder, and to promote the young warrior (to whom a certain sexual license was perhaps allowed, to judge from the episode of the naked women cited above) into the class of married men. Only the choice of the girl is allowed him, and he chooses Emer, the daughter of Forgall Manach. Her father opposes the marriage, for no apparent reason except the ritual conventions which require that every marriage shall be an abduction. He imposes upon the warrior a further apprenticeship in warfare in the form of a visit to Scáthach ('The Shadowy One'), who dwells in the Alps (*Alpi*), or, as others say, in Scotland (*Albu*), in

[1] Thurneysen, *op. cit.*, 377.

those mysterious borders of the world which the myth peoples with supernatural beings.

Cú Chulainn sets out with two companions, who soon abandon him, in retreat before the terrors of these inhuman regions. The hero is the eternal solitary, he who perseveres when others turn back. Through one adventure after another, escorted by monsters, guided by talismans, crossing on a slender cord an abyss peopled with phantoms, he arrives at the gate of Scáthach's dwelling, and breaks it open with the shaft of his spear. Attracted by the hero's beauty, Uathach ('The Terrible'), daughter of Scáthach, makes him welcome. He rewards her by attacking her, breaking her finger, and killing the champion who rushes to her aid. Having been taken into service by Scáthach, he takes advantage of her, when she is instructing her two sons, to leap on to her breast and threaten her with his sword. She then grants him three wishes: she will instruct him carefully, give him her daughter without a bride-price, and foretell his future career.

Scáthach is at war with another 'queen' of this country, Aífe, of whom it is said that she cares for nothing in the world as much as for her horses and her chariot, and who is thus akin to those chariot-goddesses whom we have already encountered. Cú Chulainn conquers her by a stratagem and forces her too to grant him three wishes: she will be the vassal of Scáthach, she will sleep one night with him, and will bear him a son. This son is Conláech, whom his father later kills in single combat without knowing him. Finally, when he has finished his apprenticeship with Scáthach (the saga gives a list of the *clessa* that he has learnt from her), the hero sets out for home. Before escaping from this fantastic kingdom, he has to slay another female demon, Éis Énchenn ('Birdhead'), an old woman blind of the left eye, like the daughters of Calatin whom we shall hear of later.

Thus the hero's military training, which began within the tribe, is completed at the court of formidable queens, who are both teachers and warriors, sisters of the mother-goddesses, of Anu who 'nourishes the gods', and of the *Badb*, the chariot-goddess, the raven-goddess. The nature of his connection with these female powers is double: he overcomes them by violence, and he is sexually united with them, a double relationship between man and the supernatural powers which we have already observed in the myths of the mother-goddesses and in the encounters between the race of men and the people of the *Síde*. Thus the men of Ireland reduce Carman to slavery; the Dagda is united to the *Morrígan*; the companions of Nera break into the *Síd* and plunder it, and Nera takes a wife there. Violence or hierogamy are the two means by which man can break down the barrier which separates the two worlds so as to make contact with the supernatural powers, bring them under his control, and make them serve his purpose.

After his return, Cú Chulainn tries for a whole year in vain to enter the dwelling of Emer. Finally one day he arrives in his scythed chariot, performs the 'feat of thunder of three hundred and nine men', kills with three thrusts of his spear three times eight men, who are comrades of Emer's three brothers, without harming the brothers themselves, and leaps over the triple rampart of the fort of Forgall. Forgall tries to leap over the rampart and is killed. Cú Chulainn re-crosses the triple rampart at a single bound, bearing with him Emer, her weight in gold, and her foster-sister. The abduction of the fostersister may be a survival of group-marriage, the family giving the bridegroom secondary wives in addition to the chief spouse. The legend of Conchobor,[1] husband of the four daughters of Eochaid Feidlech, Mumain, Eithne, Clothra and the famous queen Medb, preserves, perhaps, a trace of an analogous system

[1] Thurneysen, *op. cit.*, 531.

of marriage, which combines polygyny with monogamy, as practised, for example, in ancient Chinese society.[1]

The hero's marriage leads him into conflict with tribal law again, and again the law bends before him without breaking. It is the custom that the first night of the bride belongs to the king. But Cú Chulainn, who is accustomed to be first everywhere, is provoked to the violent fury to which he is subject. To calm him they resort to an expedient. He is sent to collect the herds of the province. He returns driving before him all the wild animals of Ulster. Meanwhile the sages have planned a compromise. The king cannot renounce his right without violating one of his *geasa*. He will spend the night with Emer, but Fergus and the druid Cathbad will spend the night with them to guard the honour of Cú Chulainn. Nevertheless, he receives his honour-price in the morning, and in addition he is awarded supremacy over all the young men of Ulster, including the king's sons.

A violent death is the necessary crowning of the hero's career. Incarnating all human values, and charged with the whole burden of human destiny, he finds completion only in death. And yet his death raises a problem. How shall the invincible hero die undefeated? What force can break him without lessening his greatness? All the epic legends encounter the same difficulty, and all avoid it by the same device, namely by introducing a force that is not of heroic quality, even opposed to the heroic quality, so that the hero is not defeated on his own ground, but becomes a victim of trickery so that his defeat does not count. In a world dominated by warlike notions, this anti-heroic force is betrayal: thus Roland is betrayed by Ganelon, and Achilles is struck from behind. In a world dominated by notions of magic, this force is sorcery: Cú Chulainn is conquered by sorcerers who know how to use against him

[1] M. Granet, *La Société chinoise*, 411.

the only force that can break him, his own destiny, or, in Celtic terminology, his *geasa*.

The circumstances of his death illustrate a certain mechanism of magic which is specifically Celtic, and it is worth while to recall them in detail.[1]

Cú Chulainn had killed Calatin the Brave and his twenty-seven sons long before. But his wife had borne six posthumous children at one birth, three sons and three daughters. Queen Medb, planning the hero's death, made these children into sorcerers. For that purpose the right foot and the left hand of the sons are cut off and the left eye of each of the daughters is blinded, an initiatory mutilation of magicians of which we heard an echo in other myths (pp. 5 and 34). So also Odin paid with one of his eyes for his knowledge of runes. For seventeen years the children of Calatin go through the world learning magic. For seven years the sons forge magic spears, to be instruments of their vengeance. Then Medb assembles the four provinces of Ireland to invade the country of Cú Chulainn, and the 'Great Carnage of Mag Muirthemne' begins. Unhindered by the insistence of his people or by evil omens, the hero rushes into battle. He meets on the way the three daughters of Calatin who are roasting a dog on a branch of rowan and singing incantations. Now it is *geis* for him to pass a hearth without tasting the food that is being prepared, but it is also *geis* for him to eat the flesh of the dog, his namesake and perhaps his totem. He is thus caught between two of his *geasa*, 'overtaken by his *geasa*', as king Conaire said. He takes the dog's shoulder that is offered him and places it under his left thigh: his hand and his thigh wither immediately.

The hero, although now virtually undone, is still formidable. In order to disarm him, his enemies resort to one of the most deadly magic powers known to the Celt, the power

[1] Thurneysen, *op. cit.*, 547.

of the word, the weapon of the poets, who can take away
the honour or the life of anyone who denies what they
ask, by means of their satire (*áer*). When he reaches the
field of battle, Cú Chulainn meets a 'chanter' who demands
his spear, threatening to satirize him if he refuses. The
hero throws him his spear, but in such a way that it pierces
him and nine men behind him. Lugaid, an enemy warrior,
then casts the first spear forged by the sons of Calatin, but
succeeds only in killing Láeg the charioteer. Cú Chulainn
takes the spear out of the body and is armed again. To a
second chanter, who demands this second spear, he replies
that he is bound to grant only one request each day in
order to protect his honour. The sorcerer then threatens
to satirize the men of Ulster. Now we know that this
hero is the guardian of his people's honour. He throws
away the second spear for the sake of the honour of his
province, and then, in similar circumstances, a third for
the honour of his race. Lugaid then succeeds in wounding
his disarmed adversary, whose entrails gush forth into the
chariot.

Here the dramatic instinct which is revealed in all this
epic tradition has contrived an effective pause in the midst
of the fracas of the 'Great Carnage'. Cú Chulainn asks
his adversaries to allow him to go to the lake for a drink.
Gathering up his entrails, he goes down to the water,
drinks there and washes himself. When a 'water-dog' (an
otter) comes to drink his blood, which has reddened the
lake, he kills it with a cast from his sling. He knows then
that his end has come, for it was foretold to him that his
first exploit and his last would be the death of a dog.
Summoning his enemies, he defies them until 'his sight
darkens'. He binds himself then with his belt to a pillar-
stone so that he may die standing, while the Grey of Macha,
his horse, protects him in his agony, making 'three red
charges' in which it kills fifty men with its teeth and

thirty with its hooves. Only when a crow perches on his shoulder and the 'hero's moon' fades from his forehead, does Lugaid dare to approach and cut off his head. His sword then falls from his hand and severs Lugaid's arm. The right hand is cut from the hero's body as a reprisal, and the head and hand are carried off to Tara.

Conall Cernach, brother in arms of Cú Chulainn, makes haste to recover the bloody trophy. He pursues the enemy, kills Lugaid, and recovers the head, which is placed upon a rock, and splits it, burying itself deep in the stone, in a final manifestation of that ardour, in the most physical sense of the word, which emanates from the hero. Conall then brings the head to Emer, together with a whole garland of enemy heads strung on an osier withe. Cú Chulainn is avenged, and his widow must now abide with him in death. Conall digs a deep grave, and Emer lies upon the dead body, places her lips on the lips of the severed head, and dies. Conall erects a stone bearing an inscription in ogam, and utters the funeral lament. The career of the hero, chief of the warriors of Ulster, defender of the tribe, is at an end. This happened on the day of the feast of *Samain*.

CHAPTER VII

THE HEROES OUTSIDE THE TRIBE

Passing from the legend of Cú Chulainn to the legends of the *Fiana*, one has the impression of entering a heroic world which is not only different from that in which the tribal hero moves, but irreconcilable with it. The two bodies of tradition have some conceptions in common: the same fusion of warrior and magician in the person of hero-magicians, the same constant coming and going between the world of men and the world of the *Síde*, between sacred and profane. But in other respects the contrast seems complete. It is not merely a difference of formal character, details of manners, technique of warfare, here on foot or on horseback, there in a chariot; it is a difference of function, which is more important, of the position which the hero occupies in society and in the world. Cú Chulainn finds his place quite naturally, though it is a dominant place, in Celtic society as we know it not only from the sagas but from history. He has his fort at Dún Delgan, his domain of Mag Muirthemne, his appointed place at the king's knee among the other heroes, the first among them, it is true, but *primus inter pares.* Finn with his bands of warriors (*fiana*) is by definition outside the tribal institutions: he is the living negation of the spirit which dominates them. The two mythologies present two independent conceptions of the hero. They do not conflict. They are unaware of each other. How can they have existed together among the same people at the same time?

The name *fian* ('warrior-band')[1] corresponds etymologically to Old Slavonic *vojna* 'war' and belongs to the root
from which are derived Latin *uēnāri* 'to hunt', Avestic
vanaiti 'conquers, obtains by force', Sanskrit *vanóti* 'wins,
conquers', *vanús* 'warrior', Old High German *winnan* 'to
fight', etc., and which expresses the notion of 'conquering,
acquiring by warfare or hunting'. The *fian* was then originally a band of men who lived by hunting and plunder.
What the epic legends tell us about the *fiana* confirms what
the etymology suggests.

The *fiana* are companies of hunting warriors, living as
semi-nomads under the authority of their own leaders.
They are represented as spending the season of hunting
and warfare (from *Beltine* to *Samain*) roaming the forests
of Ireland in pursuit of game, or as guerillas. The later
tales present them as the appointed defenders of their
country against foreign invaders, but this is clearly a
secondary development. During the winter season, from
Samain to *Beltine*, they live mainly off the country like
billeted troops. They are not under obedience to the
king, with whom their leaders are often in conflict. Of
these leaders the most popular is Finn, leader of the Clanna
Baoiscne, the *fiana* of Leinster, who is said to have died
in the latter half of the third century A.D. at the age of
two hundred and thirty. Finn is the father of Oisín, or
Ossian, from whom the cycle of the *fiana* is called the
Ossianic cycle. Variant traditions which have been eclipsed
by the growing popularity of Finn, gave the highest
honour to other leaders such as Goll, leader of the *fiana*
of Connaught.

The *fiana* are not a race, nor are they tribes in the
ordinary sense of the word, nor are they, strictly speaking,
a caste. One is not born a *féinid*, or member of the *fian*;
one acquires that status by choice. And one must satisfy

[1] Meyer, *Fianaigecht*, p. vi.

rigorous requirements. The candidate must have an advanced liberal education, being versed in the twelve traditional forms of poetry; and the heroes of the *fiana* are poets as well as warriors. A great number of poems are attributed to Finn, the *ríg-fhéinid* ('king-*féinid*'), to his son Oisín and his adopted son Caílte. Moreover, the candidate must successfully undergo a series of ritual ordeals, analogous to the ordeals of initiation which candidates undergo before admission into the secret societies or fraternities which play so large a part among many primitive or semi-primitive peoples[1]. The ordeals are as follows:[2] a hole is dug in the ground deep enough for a man to be buried in it to his waist. The candidate takes his place there armed only with his shield and a stick of hazel as long as his forearm. The nine warriors throw their javelins at him together. If one javelin touches him, he is not accepted into the *fian*. Then he must braid his hair and make his way through the forest. All the warriors pursue him, seeking to wound him. If he is caught, or if his weapons have trembled in his hands, or if a dead branch has cracked under his foot, or if a live branch has disturbed a single braid of his hair, he is not accepted. He must be able to draw a thorn out of his foot without slowing his speed, and leap over a hurdle as high as his forehead and pass under a hurdle as low as his knee.

From the day when, having fulfilled all these requirements, he is received as a *féinid*, he breaks all connection with his own clan. The members of his clan must pledge themselves not to claim compensation for his death or for any injury he may suffer, and he is not bound to avenge wrongs done to the clan.[3] He is outside the system of

---

[1] There is a useful summary of the facts concerning these fraternities in H. Jeanmaire, *Couroi et Courètes*, 186.

[2] S. H. O'Grady, *Silva Gadelica*, ii, 100.

[3] *ib.* 99-100. The text says: 'and if they commit crimes, their clans are not liable for compensation' [Tr.].

collective responsibility which is the juridical expression of
the unity of the clan. He is *écland* ('clanless'), and has no
other kindred, no social group save the *fian*. While the
féinid is outside the tribe, he is not on that account outside
the law, for the law recognizes his position, and treats
him as an outsider, not as a pariah.[1] The depredations that
he does, which are in fact necessary to his subsistence, for
as an *écland* he is also *díthír* ('landless'), are legal and he is
never represented as a brigand. No longer protected by
his people, nor by their law, he at once acquires the right
to secure justice for himself. 'Reprisals' are an appanage
of the *féinid* just as hostages are an appanage of the king,
says one of the texts. And it is an axiom of the law that
'a king is not a king without hostages'. More than that,
the *fiana* are not merely tolerated, they are counted among
the institutions necessary to the prosperity of the tribe
provided that they are 'without excess', that is to say,
provided that they restrict themselves within certain limits.
Their members have a certain claim on the community:
not only do they live off the people during the winter
season, but they have a right of option upon the women
of the tribe. No girl may be given in marriage until she
has been offered to the *fiana*, an exorbitant privilege, and
one that did not go unchallenged, if we are to believe
the legend which says that it was the origin of their ruin.
The king of Ireland Cairbre wished to marry his daughter
Sgéimh Sholais ('Beauty of Light') to a prince, and the
fiana opposed the marriage, claiming the girl for one of
themselves or the payment of a ransom of twenty ounces
of gold. The enraged Cairbre resolved to destroy their
power, and gave them battle at Gabhair (283 A.D.) where
he lost his life but inflicted upon his enemies such losses
that they never recovered.

The *féinid* lives on the margin of society, in forest and

[1] Meyer, *Fianaigecht*, p. ix.

wilderness where the tribal hero adventures only on brief expeditions, the domain of the *Tuatha*, of the people of the *Síde*, the Celtic spirits of the wilderness. He is in constant contact with those mysterious powers which the man who dwells within the tribe, upon the tribal land and close to the hearth, encounters only rarely, in the chaos of *Samain*-eve or by favour of an initiation from the Otherworld. Thus the myths of the *fiana* take us directly into the region of the supernatural.

Living on the margin of human affairs, as advanced outposts of the natural world in the supernatural world, the heroes of the *fiana* have a part in both these worlds and a double character.

These heroes, therefore, show traces of that semi-animal nature, proper to a fluid mythical world in which the species are not separated by rigid distinctions, and which we have seen to be the appanage of various divinities. One of the wives of Finn (for Finn, in contrast to the monogamous Cú Chulainn, has a whole series of wives) is a doe named Saar.[1] Her child will be a human, if the doe does not lick it: if she does it will be a fawn. The doe does not resist the impulse to lick the infant on the forehead, and that is why Oisín has a tuft of fur on his forehead. His name means 'little fawn'. Finn's two dogs, Bran and Sgeolán, his most faithful companions, are his own nephews, sons of his sister Tuirenn who had been changed into a bitch by a jealous rival[2]—or so the folklore explains by magic the existence in the same family of different animal species, a phenomenon which requires no explanation to a primitive mind.[3] Finn himself betrays this double nature, for he was dog, man or deer, according to the way he wore his magic hood.[4] He even possesses

[1] Campbell, *Leabhar na Feinne*, 198.
[2] *Trans. Oss. Soc.*, ii, 161-7. The text says that Tuirenn was a sister of Finn's mother [Tr.].
[3] Lévy-Bruhl, *Mythologie primitive*, 35, *et pass.*
[4] Meyer, *Fianaigecht*, 51.

the faculty of assuming any animal form, not indeed as Finn but as king Mongán, if we are to accept the tradition which makes this king a re-incarnation of Finn, stating that Mongán was Finn, 'although he would not let it be told'.[1] We have seen that another tradition represents Mongán to be the son of Manannán (s. p. 46). Thus mythology sets him in relationship by transformation either with the god of the sea, who belongs to the same class as the mother-goddesses (p. 46), or with one of the heroes of the *fiana*, who have the same semi-animal nature as those goddesses, like them inhabiting the wilderness where the conditions of the mythological period still prevail, and immersed in the fluidity of a primitive world from which the chieftain-gods and the tribal hero have become separated.

To recount the exploits of the *fiana* and summarize the tales which describe them would be to repeat much of what has been said about the cycle of Cú Chulainn and would also lead us almost inevitably beyond the limits of Celtic mythology into questions of international folklore which we have sought to avoid. Leaving aside secondary developments of the cycle, literary or popular, we shall consider only the fundamental problem which it presents. What are the *fiana*? Are they a social institution or a mythological notion, or both at the same time by transposition on to the mythological plane of a fact of history?

The Irish annalists admit as a matter of course the historicity of the Fenian Cycle. For the historian Keating (17th cent.) the *fiana* are a professional army charged with the defence of the country against foreign invasion. This conception prevails in the most recent stories, but it does not correspond to conditions reflected by the earlier texts, in which the *fiana* appear constantly at war with each other or with the royal power, and assume no national function. And what we know of Irish history does not suggest the

[1] Meyer, *Imram Brain*, i, 52.

existence of a regular army charged with the defence of the country.

A second theory is that proposed by Zimmer, who attributed a Scandinavian origin to the cycle.[1] The legends of the *fiana* would have developed around the chieftains and the mighty deeds of Viking bands established in Ireland. But the hypothesis rests on very hazardous foundations, and, moreover, it is contradicted by the antiquity of this body of legends whose popularity is attested from as early as the seventh century, while the Vikings do not appear upon the coasts of Ireland till the end of the eighth century. Zimmer's theory is useful only for the analogies it presents between the world of the *fiana* and certain aspects of the heroic world of Scandinavian tradition, analogies which are to be explained not as loans but from the common origin of religious ideas in correlation with a particular social order, Celtic on the one hand and Germanic on the other. It is not by comparison with the Vikings who invaded Ireland in the ninth century that Fenian mythology can be explained, but by comparison with the myths of the *Einherjar*, the chosen of Odin, or with the savage *Berserkir*, the 'bearskin warriors'.[2] On both sides we find the same violent life, on the margin of ordered society, the same fury, the same personalities with animal components and the same type of warlike fraternities.

The fact that myths comparable to those of the *fiana* are found in the Germanic world obliges us to use caution in considering a later explanation of the Celtic tradition which Eoin Mac Neill put forward,[3] although it is attractive. He seeks the origin of the Fenian Cycle among those indigenous peoples who inhabited pre-Celtic Ireland, according to the *Book of Conquests*, and whose descendants

---

[1] *Zeitschr. f. deutsches Alterthum*, 35, 1 f. and 252 f.

[2] Lily Weiser, *Kultische Geheimbünde der Germanen*; G. Dumézil, *Mythes et Dieux des Germains*, 79.

[3] *Duanaire Finn*, I, p. xxiv.

constitute in the historic period the *aithech-thuatha* ('serf tribes'). This theory would explain one matter with regard to the literary development of the two cycles, namely the small place filled in our earliest manuscript collections by the legends of the *fiana*, although they are as ancient as the legends of Cú Chulainn, and were destined to enjoy a popularity as great and even more lasting. This temporary suppression would be due to the contempt of the dominant class for the myths of subject peoples, and would have ceased at a time when racial distinctions had diminished, and diverse political changes had favoured the passage into aristocratic and literary tradition of a body of legend which had been until then relegated to the oral tradition of the unfree classes.

It is *a priori* probable, as we shall see, that the dispossessed classes played a part in the elaboration and diffusion of these myths, and certain indications confirm this view. Many of the numerous genealogies of Finn make him a *Fer Bolg*. But the striking analogy between the Celtic and Germanic mythologies, which cannot be held apart, postulates an Indo-European origin. Thus it is in terms of the Celtic world that we must explain this type of mythological presentation, and it is to the Celtic world that we must attribute the dualism which comprises in addition to the tribal hero, the hero outside the tribe.

Perhaps if we examine the native tradition, accepting quite simply the facts as it presents them, it will furnish the solution of the problem. The Fenian hero Caílte tells the nobles of Ireland that king Feradach Fechtnach had two sons, Tuathal and Fiacha.[1] When he died, his sons divided Ireland into two parts (as the *Tuatha Dé Danann* and the Sons of Míl had done before): one took 'the treasure, the herds and the fortresses', and the other 'the cliffs and estuaries, the fruits of forest and sea, the salmon and the game'.

[1] Standish H. O'Grady, *Silva Gadelica*, ii, 165.

The nobles interrupt Caílte, protesting against the inequality of this division. 'Which of the two parts would you have chosen?' asks Oisín, son of Finn. 'The banquets, the dwellings and all the other precious things,' say the nobles. 'The part that you despise,' says Caílte, 'seems more precious to us.' This was indeed the opinion of the younger son, who 'chose to throw in his lot with the *fiana*', while his brother inherited the sovranty of Ireland. On the death of this brother he was to succeed to the kingdom, leaving to someone else the command of the *fiana*.

We see that the good things of this world fall into two parts: all that is subject to man and fruit of his work belongs to the tribe and to those who live under its laws; wild nature belongs to the *féinid*, and is the land of the landless. In one family vocation may decide which of the brothers shall be king and which shall become a *féinid*.

Other motives than vocation may intervene to prompt a hero, or even a heroine, 'to throw in his lot with the *fiana*'. We have an instance in the story of Créidne.[1] Créidne had three sons by her own father, the king of Ireland. Fearing the displeasure of his wife, he expelled the children 'from his land and kindred'; and Créidne, to avenge this wrong upon her father and her stepmother, went *for fiannas*. 'She had three companies of nine men on the warpath with her. She fought on sea as well as on land, and wore her hair in braids. That is why men called her Créidne the *féinid*.' She spent seven years in this way on campaigns in Ireland and Scotland before making peace with her father.

We see that the *fiana* are established side by side with the tribe, and draw upon it, attracting its abnormal elements, all those individuals who feel out of place, or who have no place, within the tribe. But they are not mere aggregates of asocial elements; it is not enough that one be

[1] Meyer, *Fianaigecht*, p. xii.

outside the tribe to be in the *fian*, for admission is restricted by rigorous ordeals. The *fiana* constitute a society independent of tribal society and resting on a basis, not of family or territory, but of initiation. The non-Celtic element of the population, since they found themselves by definition excluded from the closed tribal society, must have contributed largely to the formation of this other society which was recruited openly and free from racial discrimination. But we have seen that the younger son of a royal family could choose the lot of the *féinid*, and that he did not thereby forfeit the right to return into the society to which he belonged by birth. The *fiana* were not groups of subject aliens, a theory which accords ill with the prestige and the privileges they enjoyed; they were fraternities of a type which is known elsewhere in the Indo-European world, and which were regarded as in some measure necessary to the well-being of Celtic society.

Every society, and specially a closed society organized in rigid classes, like that of the Celts, includes certain abnormal elements for which allowance must be made. These elements tend naturally to integrate themselves with the *fiana*, whose life was one of regulated irregularity. Thus Celtic society provides its own antidote, and copes with what is asocial by expelling it, while at the same time recognizing its right and assigning to it a particular domain.

One can grasp the meaning and functional justification of the dualism which dominates the heroic world of Ireland. The myth of Cú Chulainn is the myth of the tribal man, the exaltation of heroism as a social function. The myth of the *fiana* is the myth of man outside the tribe, the release of gratuitous heroism. These two conceptions do not contradict each other, but form an opposition like thesis and antithesis, two complementary aspects of the racial temperament. The social seal which marks the two cycles from the beginning explains their later destiny. The myth of Cú Chulainn, a heritage of ordered society, of princes, scholars and clerics, after dominating for a long time the literary tradition of the propertied classes, declined and disappeared with that society and those classes. The myth of the *fiana*, relegated for centuries to the shadow of oral tradition, shares the longevity of folk-lore and survives to this day in the folktales of the people.

CONCLUSION

I N travelling through the dense forest of the insular legends,
and stirring the ashes of the continental Celtic world,
we did not hope to uncover the plan of a vast edifice, a
temple of the Celtic gods, partly overrun by the luxuriant
wilderness and partly ruined by invaders. The indications
are that this edifice never existed. Other people raised
temples to their gods, and their very mythologies are
temples whose architecture reproduces the symmetry of a
cosmic or social order—an order both cosmic and social.
It is in the wild solitude of the νεμητον, the sacred woodland,
that the Celtic tribe meets its gods, and its mythical world
is a sacred forest, pathless and unbounded, which is inhabited by mysterious powers. Against these powers, man,
situated in the midst of the supernatural, and himself
possessed by it, defends with difficulty by force or by magic
his small domain, which is always surrounded by invisible
tribes and subject on certain ritual days to direct invasion.

Hence the uneasiness we feel in approaching this world:
we seek for a cosmos and find chaos. A mixture of races,
human and divine, a multitude of ill-defined mythological
figures, whose activities are not clearly differentiated, share
amongst themselves or contend for a land which we can
hardly recognize as ours, a world which is indeed our
world but pregnant with many 'otherworlds'.

For the Celt imagines his gods as dwelling on this earth.
For him there is no 'beyond' or 'elsewhere', no reservation
to which he can relegate what is sacred, whether for
reasons of respect or of prudence. He is encamped upon a
soil that was contoured of old by his great mythical
ancestors, and formerly under the sway of the Tribes of

the Goddess Dana. To-day it is divided between two camps, the camp of men and the other camp. In this other camp are the supernatural powers, of whom man has made himself diverse images, among which there appear two dominant types as leit-motivs of Celtic religious thought, a female type and a male type. The female type is that of the mother-goddess, single and triple, local divinities, river-goddesses, goddesses of seasonal feasts, animal goddesses, mothers and teachers, incarnations of natural forces of fertility or destruction, for the series of 'mothers' merges into that of goddesses of slaughter so that one cannot establish a clear opposition between them. This is true at least of the insular tradition which is more archaic in this respect than that of the continent. The male type is that of the chief god, the Dagda or Sucellos, father, nurturer, protector of the tribe, warrior, magician and craftsman, the Teutates of universal activity and total efficiency.

Thus we have a male principle of society to which is opposed a female principle of nature, or rather (for it is important that we do not find an abstract unity in what the Celt conceived as a concrete multiplicity) social forces of male character opposed by natural forces of female character. Other Indo-European peoples have projected into this eschatology the scheme of a differentiated society, dividing specialized functions and activities among their gods; and Celtic mythology shows traces of such a division, but it has been relegated to a position of secondary importance by the opposition between the social group and its environment, between human activity, one and undifferentiated, and the forces of nature which it must master or conciliate. The union of the god of the tribe with the goddess of the earth, of Sucellos with Nantosuelta, of the Dagda with the *Morrígan* or with Boann, projects on the plane of mythology what the union of the king with the animal incarnation of the goddess realizes on the plane of ritual, namely the marriage of the human group with the fertile soil, which is the necessary condition for the prosperity of the tribe and the purpose of all religious activity.

In the camp of men is the Hero, the incarnation of the talents necessary to a race which lives in a world saturated with magic, warlike talents but also magical talents. The Celtic hero, whether he is called Finn or Cú Chulainn the *siabartha* ('demoniacal'), is partly a magician, or, if one prefers, a sorcerer (*shaman*). Neither in the human world nor in the divine are magician and warrior opposed to each other. All is magic, and no activity can be effective unless it has an element of magic. Irish mythology presents two realizations of the heroic type, and they are two complementary aspects of the same force, the social and the asocial, the normal and the irregular. On the one hand we have the hero in the service of the tribe, and on the other the heroes outside the tribe. And this dualism reproduces, in some degree, in the camp of men, the dualism we have observed in the camp of the gods, opposing heroism as a social function to heroism as a natural force. In many respects Cú Chulainn may be compared to the chiefs and champions of the gods, while the heroes of the *fiana* share in the eternal and changing quality of the deities of the forest and the waters.

Behind these complexes of mythology, and in correlation with them, one discerns a series of ritual complexes, of which some continued for a long time to play a large part in the life of Christian Ireland, while others shared the decline of the ancient gods: seasonal fertility festivals celebrated in holy places in honour of the mother-goddesses; the ritual of warriors, sacrifices of fire and water, the drinking and hierogamy of the feast of the new year; tribal initiation, of which traces survive in the legend of Cú

Chulainn; initiation into fraternities, attested in the Fenian legends—a whole system of magic which is akin in many respects to that which has been observed in so-called primitive societies and differs from that which prevailed in the greater part of the Indo-European domain.

BIBLIOGRAPHY

THIS brief bibliography is intended merely to enable the reader to obtain a general view of the subject. It includes only the principal works or discussions of general importance, the collections of texts, and some separate tales which have been translated and are accessible to French readers.

GENERAL

G. Roth, *Mythologie Celtique* in F. Guiraud, *Mythologie Générale* (Larousse, 1935), pp. 201 et seq. (Some errors regarding the insular Celtic tradition.)

Most of the known facts have been collected by J. A. MacCulloch, *The Religion of the Ancient Celts*, Edinburgh, 1911, and *Celtic Mythology*, Boston, 1918. His interpretation of the facts is often doubtful. The *Celtic Mythology* contains a good bibliography. H. Hubert, *Les Celtes depuis l'époque de la Tène et la civilisation celtique* (Paris, 1932), 273, contains a suggestive and enlightening discussion of Celtic religion and the priesthood of the druids. A.G. van Hamel, *Aspects of Celtic Mythology* (*Proc. Brit. Acad.* xx, 207) expresses original opinions.

For the religion of the continental Celts, s. C. Clemen, *Religionsgeschichte Europas* (Heidelberg, 1926), I, 314. G. Dottin, *Manuel pour servir à l'étude de l'antiquité celtique* (2nd ed., Paris, 1913), may still be consulted with profit. Camille Jullian, *Histoire de la Gaule*, I, 84; 113, is sometimes subject to caution.

For the religion and folklore of the insular Celts, E. Hull, *Folklore of the British Isles* (London, 1928), and T. Gwynn Jones, *Welsh Folklore and Folk Custom* (London, 1928) supply a good collection of well-verified facts.

A general study of the Irish mythological cycle is D'Arbois de Jubainville, *The Irish Mythological Cycle*, trsl. with additional notes by R. I. Best (Dublin, 1903), which is now antiquated but has not been replaced; A. Nutt, *Voyage of Bran*, I *The Happy Otherworld*; II *The Celtic Doctrine of Rebirth* (London 1895, 1897) discusses Celtic notions of the other world: antiquated and often untrustworthy.

For heroic legends, s. Czarnowski, *Le Culte des héros et ses conditions sociales* (Paris, 1919), with an excellent preface by H. Hubert; for the cycle of Cú Chulainn, s. R. Thurneysen, *Die irische Helden- und Königsage*, Halle, 1921, a masterpiece of exact workmanship, but without any discussion of mythological problems, and Windisch's introduction to *Die altirische Heldensage Táin Bó Cualnge* (Leipzig, 1905); for the cycle of the *fiana*, the introduction by E. MacNeill to his edition of *Duanaire Finn* (London, 1908) may be consulted. E. Hull, *A Textbook of Irish Literature*, II, gives a summary of the whole cycle and of the theories which have been proposed concerning it.

COLLECTIONS

For Gaulish names and titles s. A. Holder, *Altkeltischer Sprachschatz* (Leipzig, 1896–1907); for classical texts concerning Celtic religion, Johannes Zwicker, *Fontes Historiae Religionis Celticae* (three fasciculi, Bonn 1934–36); for Irish texts, R. I. Best, *Bibliography of Irish Philology and of printed Irish Literature* (Dublin, 1913), 78, and *Bibliography of Irish Philology and Manuscript Literature 1913–1941* (Dublin, 1942), 68. *The Encyclopædia of Religion and Ethics* contains a number of articles dealing with Celtic matters.

TEXTS

W. Krause, *Die Kelten* (Tübingen, 1929. *Religionsgeschichtliches Lesebuch*, 13) is a good little anthology of texts concerning Celtic mythology. For Irish traditions of the mythological period see W. Stokes, 'The Second Battle of Moytura', *Revue Celtique*, 12, 52; 'The Prose Tales in the Rennes Dindshenchas', *Revue Celtique*, 15, 272; 418; 16, 31; 135; 269; E. Gwynn, *Poems from the Dindshenchas* (Royal Irish Academy, Todd Lectures Series vii) and *The Metrical Dindshenchas* (Royal Irish Academy, Todd Lectures Series ix–xii); R. A. S. Macalister and J. MacNeill, *Leabhar Gabhála, The Book of Conquests of Ireland* (Dublin, n. d.); R. A. S. Macalister, *Lebor Gabála Erenn, The Book of the Taking of Ireland*, I–IV (Irish Texts Society xxxiv–v, xxxix, xli); W. Stokes and E. Windisch, *Cóir Anmann* (*Irische Texte* III, 2, Leipzig, 1897). All these editions include good English translations.

There is a detailed analysis of all the texts of the cycle of Cú Chulainn in R. Thurneysen, *Die irische Helden- und Königsage*, already mentioned. See also d'Arbois de Jubainville, *Táin Bó Cúalnge, Enlèvement des vaches de Cooley* (Paris, 1907), and *l'Épopée celtique en Irlande* (*Cours de littérature celtique*, v, Paris, 1892 (a free translation, not always exact); J. Dunn, *The Ancient Epic Tale, Táin Bó Cúalnge*, 'The Cúalnge Cattle-Raid' (London, 1914); G. Dottin, *L'Épopée irlandaise* (Paris, 1926, a small collection of exact translations); R. Chauviré, *La Geste de la Branche Rouge* (Paris, 1926, a literary adaptation); T. P. Cross and C. H. Slover, *Ancient Irish Tales* (London, 1936).

There are English translations of the chief texts of the Fenian cycle in K. Meyer, *Fianaigecht* (Royal Irish Academy Todd Lectures Series xvi); S. H. O'Grady, *Silva Gadelica* (London, 1892), II, 96 (a free rendering and partly out of date); E. MacNeill, *Duanaire Finn* (Irish Texts Society vii) G. Murphy, *Duanaire Finn* II (Irish Texts Society xxviii); For Scottish traditions concerning Finn and the *fiana*, see J. F. Campbell, *Leabhar na Feinne* (London, 1872) and R. T. Christiansen, *The Vikings and the Viking Wars in Irish and Gaelic Tradition* (Oslo, 1931).

Welsh texts: see J. Loth, *Les Mabinogion* I and II (Paris, 1913), which contains a masterly translation of the Middle Welsh epic tales, a collection of triads (II, 223), and many notes on British mythology; T. P. Ellis and John Lloyd, *The Mabinogion* (London, 1929); Gwyn Jones and Thomas Jones, *The Mabinogion* (London, 1948).

INDEXES

NAMES OF PERSONS

NAMES OF PLACES AND RIVERS

IRISH WORDS, Etc.

TITLES

A CATALOG OF SELECTED DOVER
BOOKS IN ALL FIELDS OF INTEREST

CONCERNING THE SPIRITUAL IN ART, Wassily Kandinsky. Pioneering work by father of abstract art. Thoughts on color theory, nature of art. Analysis of earlier masters. 12 illustrations. 80pp. of text. 5⅜ x 8½. 23411-8

ANIMALS: 1,419 Copyright-Free Illustrations of Mammals, Birds, Fish, Insects, etc., Jim Harter (ed.). Clear wood engravings present, in extremely lifelike poses, over 1,000 species of animals. One of the most extensive pictorial sourcebooks of its kind. Captions. Index. 284pp. 9 x 12. 23766-4

CELTIC ART: The Methods of Construction, George Bain. Simple geometric techniques for making Celtic interlacements, spirals, Kells-type initials, animals, humans, etc. Over 500 illustrations. 160pp. 9 x 12. (Available in U.S. only.) 22923-8

AN ATLAS OF ANATOMY FOR ARTISTS, Fritz Schider. Most thorough reference work on art anatomy in the world. Hundreds of illustrations, including selections from works by Vesalius, Leonardo, Goya, Ingres, Michelangelo, others. 593 illustrations. 192pp. 7⅛ x 10¼. 20241-0

CELTIC HAND STROKE-BY-STROKE (Irish Half-Uncial from "The Book of Kells"): An Arthur Baker Calligraphy Manual, Arthur Baker. Complete guide to creating each letter of the alphabet in distinctive Celtic manner. Covers hand position, strokes, pens, inks, paper, more. Illustrated. 48pp. 8¼ x 11. 24336-2

EASY ORIGAMI, John Montroll. Charming collection of 32 projects (hat, cup, pelican, piano, swan, many more) specially designed for the novice origami hobbyist. Clearly illustrated easy-to-follow instructions insure that even beginning papercrafters will achieve successful results. 48pp. 8¼ x 11. 27298-2

THE COMPLETE BOOK OF BIRDHOUSE CONSTRUCTION FOR WOOD-WORKERS, Scott D. Campbell. Detailed instructions, illustrations, tables. Also data on bird habitat and instinct patterns. Bibliography. 3 tables. 63 illustrations in 15 figures. 48pp. 5¼ x 8½. 24407-5

BLOOMINGDALE'S ILLUSTRATED 1886 CATALOG: Fashions, Dry Goods and Housewares, Bloomingdale Brothers. Famed merchants' extremely rare catalog depicting about 1,700 products: clothing, housewares, firearms, dry goods, jewelry, more. Invaluable for dating, identifying vintage items. Also, copyright-free graphics for artists, designers. Co-published with Henry Ford Museum & Greenfield Village. 160pp. 8¼ x 11. 25780-0

HISTORIC COSTUME IN PICTURES, Braun & Schneider. Over 1,450 costumed figures in clearly detailed engravings–from dawn of civilization to end of 19th century. Captions. Many folk costumes. 256pp. 8⅜ x 11¾. 23150-X

CATALOG OF DOVER BOOKS

STICKLEY CRAFTSMAN FURNITURE CATALOGS, Gustav Stickley and L. & J. G. Stickley. Beautiful, functional furniture in two authentic catalogs from 1910. 594 illustrations, including 277 photos, show settles, rockers, armchairs, reclining chairs, bookcases, desks, tables. 183pp. 6½ x 9¼.   23838-5

AMERICAN LOCOMOTIVES IN HISTORIC PHOTOGRAPHS: 1858 to 1949, Ron Ziel (ed.). A rare collection of 126 meticulously detailed official photographs, called "builder portraits," of American locomotives that majestically chronicle the rise of steam locomotive power in America. Introduction. Detailed captions. xi+ 129pp. 9 x 12.   27393-8

AMERICA'S LIGHTHOUSES: An Illustrated History, Francis Ross Holland, Jr. Delightfully written, profusely illustrated fact-filled survey of over 200 American lighthouses since 1716. History, anecdotes, technological advances, more. 240pp. 8 x 10¾.
                                                                                                          25576-X

TOWARDS A NEW ARCHITECTURE, Le Corbusier. Pioneering manifesto by founder of "International School." Technical and aesthetic theories, views of industry, economics, relation of form to function, "mass-production split" and much more. Profusely illustrated. 320pp. 6⅛ x 9¼. (Available in U.S. only.)   25023-7

HOW THE OTHER HALF LIVES, Jacob Riis. Famous journalistic record, exposing poverty and degradation of New York slums around 1900, by major social reformer. 100 striking and influential photographs. 233pp. 10 x 7⅞.   22012-5

FRUIT KEY AND TWIG KEY TO TREES AND SHRUBS, William M. Harlow. One of the handiest and most widely used identification aids. Fruit key covers 120 deciduous and evergreen species; twig key 160 deciduous species. Easily used. Over 300 photographs. 126pp. 5⅜ x 8½.   20511-8

COMMON BIRD SONGS, Dr. Donald J. Borror. Songs of 60 most common U.S. birds: robins, sparrows, cardinals, bluejays, finches, more—arranged in order of increasing complexity. Up to 9 variations of songs of each species.
                                                                                   Cassette and manual 99911-4

ORCHIDS AS HOUSE PLANTS, Rebecca Tyson Northen. Grow cattleyas and many other kinds of orchids—in a window, in a case, or under artificial light. 63 illustrations. 148pp. 5⅜ x 8½.   23261-1

MONSTER MAZES, Dave Phillips. Masterful mazes at four levels of difficulty. Avoid deadly perils and evil creatures to find magical treasures. Solutions for all 32 exciting illustrated puzzles. 48pp. 8¼ x 11.   26005-4

MOZART'S DON GIOVANNI (DOVER OPERA LIBRETTO SERIES), Wolfgang Amadeus Mozart. Introduced and translated by Ellen H. Bleiler. Standard Italian libretto, with complete English translation. Convenient and thoroughly portable—an ideal companion for reading along with a recording or the performance itself. Introduction. List of characters. Plot summary. 121pp. 5¼ x 8½.   24944-1

TECHNICAL MANUAL AND DICTIONARY OF CLASSICAL BALLET, Gail Grant. Defines, explains, comments on steps, movements, poses and concepts. 15-page pictorial section. Basic book for student, viewer. 127pp. 5⅜ x 8½.   21843-0

THE CLARINET AND CLARINET PLAYING, David Pino. Lively, comprehensive work features suggestions about technique, musicianship, and musical interpretation, as well as guidelines for teaching, making your own reeds, and preparing for public performance. Includes an intriguing look at clarinet history. "A godsend," *The Clarinet*, Journal of the International Clarinet Society. Appendixes. 7 illus. 320pp. 5⅜ x 8½. 40270-3

HOLLYWOOD GLAMOR PORTRAITS, John Kobal (ed.). 145 photos from 1926-49. Harlow, Gable, Bogart, Bacall; 94 stars in all. Full background on photographers, technical aspects. 160pp. 8⅜ x 11¼. 23352-9

THE ANNOTATED CASEY AT THE BAT: A Collection of Ballads about the Mighty Casey/Third, Revised Edition, Martin Gardner (ed.). Amusing sequels and parodies of one of America's best-loved poems: Casey's Revenge, Why Casey Whiffed, Casey's Sister at the Bat, others. 256pp. 5⅜ x 8½. 28598-7

THE RAVEN AND OTHER FAVORITE POEMS, Edgar Allan Poe. Over 40 of the author's most memorable poems: "The Bells," "Ulalume," "Israfel," "To Helen," "The Conqueror Worm," "Eldorado," "Annabel Lee," many more. Alphabetic lists of titles and first lines. 64pp. 5$\frac{3}{16}$ x 8¼. 26685-0

PERSONAL MEMOIRS OF U. S. GRANT, Ulysses Simpson Grant. Intelligent, deeply moving firsthand account of Civil War campaigns, considered by many the finest military memoirs ever written. Includes letters, historic photographs, maps and more. 528pp. 6⅛ x 9¼. 28587-1

ANCIENT EGYPTIAN MATERIALS AND INDUSTRIES, A. Lucas and J. Harris. Fascinating, comprehensive, thoroughly documented text describes this ancient civilization's vast resources and the processes that incorporated them in daily life, including the use of animal products, building materials, cosmetics, perfumes and incense, fibers, glazed ware, glass and its manufacture, materials used in the mummification process, and much more. 544pp. 6⅛ x 9¼. (Available in U.S. only.) 40446-3

RUSSIAN STORIES/RUSSKIE RASSKAZY: A Dual-Language Book, edited by Gleb Struve. Twelve tales by such masters as Chekhov, Tolstoy, Dostoevsky, Pushkin, others. Excellent word-for-word English translations on facing pages, plus teaching and study aids, Russian/English vocabulary, biographical/critical introductions, more. 416pp. 5⅜ x 8½. 26244-8

PHILADELPHIA THEN AND NOW: 60 Sites Photographed in the Past and Present, Kenneth Finkel and Susan Oyama. Rare photographs of City Hall, Logan Square, Independence Hall, Betsy Ross House, other landmarks juxtaposed with contemporary views. Captures changing face of historic city. Introduction. Captions. 128pp. 8¼ x 11. 25790-8

AIA ARCHITECTURAL GUIDE TO NASSAU AND SUFFOLK COUNTIES, LONG ISLAND, The American Institute of Architects, Long Island Chapter, and the Society for the Preservation of Long Island Antiquities. Comprehensive, well-researched and generously illustrated volume brings to life over three centuries of Long Island's great architectural heritage. More than 240 photographs with authoritative, extensively detailed captions. 176pp. 8¼ x 11. 26946-9

NORTH AMERICAN INDIAN LIFE: Customs and Traditions of 23 Tribes, Elsie Clews Parsons (ed.). 27 fictionalized essays by noted anthropologists examine religion, customs, government, additional facets of life among the Winnebago, Crow, Zuni, Eskimo, other tribes. 480pp. 6⅛ x 9¼. 27377-6

FRANK LLOYD WRIGHT'S DANA HOUSE, Donald Hoffmann. Pictorial essay of residential masterpiece with over 160 interior and exterior photos, plans, elevations, sketches and studies. 128pp. 9¼ x 10¾. 29120-0

THE MALE AND FEMALE FIGURE IN MOTION: 60 Classic Photographic Sequences, Eadweard Muybridge. 60 true-action photographs of men and women walking, running, climbing, bending, turning, etc., reproduced from rare 19th-century masterpiece. vi + 121pp. 9 x 12. 24745-7

1001 QUESTIONS ANSWERED ABOUT THE SEASHORE, N. J. Berrill and Jacquelyn Berrill. Queries answered about dolphins, sea snails, sponges, starfish, fishes, shore birds, many others. Covers appearance, breeding, growth, feeding, much more. 305pp. 5¼ x 8¼. 23366-9

ATTRACTING BIRDS TO YOUR YARD, William J. Weber. Easy-to-follow guide offers advice on how to attract the greatest diversity of birds: birdhouses, feeders, water and waterers, much more. 96pp. 5³⁄₁₆ x 8¼. 28927-3

MEDICINAL AND OTHER USES OF NORTH AMERICAN PLANTS: A Historical Survey with Special Reference to the Eastern Indian Tribes, Charlotte Erichsen-Brown. Chronological historical citations document 500 years of usage of plants, trees, shrubs native to eastern Canada, northeastern U.S. Also complete identifying information. 343 illustrations. 544pp. 6½ x 9¼. 25951-X

STORYBOOK MAZES, Dave Phillips. 23 stories and mazes on two-page spreads: Wizard of Oz, Treasure Island, Robin Hood, etc. Solutions. 64pp. 8¼ x 11. 23628-5

AMERICAN NEGRO SONGS: 230 Folk Songs and Spirituals, Religious and Secular, John W. Work. This authoritative study traces the African influences of songs sung and played by black Americans at work, in church, and as entertainment. The author discusses the lyric significance of such songs as "Swing Low, Sweet Chariot," "John Henry," and others and offers the words and music for 230 songs. Bibliography. Index of Song Titles. 272pp. 6½ x 9¼. 40271-1

MOVIE-STAR PORTRAITS OF THE FORTIES, John Kobal (ed.). 163 glamor, studio photos of 106 stars of the 1940s: Rita Hayworth, Ava Gardner, Marlon Brando, Clark Gable, many more. 176pp. 8⅜ x 11¼. 23546-7

BENCHLEY LOST AND FOUND, Robert Benchley. Finest humor from early 30s, about pet peeves, child psychologists, post office and others. Mostly unavailable elsewhere. 73 illustrations by Peter Arno and others. 183pp. 5⅜ x 8½. 22410-4

YEKL and THE IMPORTED BRIDEGROOM AND OTHER STORIES OF YIDDISH NEW YORK, Abraham Cahan. Film Hester Street based on *Yekl* (1896). Novel, other stories among first about Jewish immigrants on N.Y.'s East Side. 240pp. 5⅜ x 8½. 22427-9

SELECTED POEMS, Walt Whitman. Generous sampling from *Leaves of Grass*. Twenty-four poems include "I Hear America Singing," "Song of the Open Road," "I Sing the Body Electric," "When Lilacs Last in the Dooryard Bloom'd," "O Captain! My Captain!"–all reprinted from an authoritative edition. Lists of titles and first lines. 128pp. 5³⁄₁₆ x 8¼. 26878-0

THE BEST TALES OF HOFFMANN, E. T. A. Hoffmann. 10 of Hoffmann's most important stories: "Nutcracker and the King of Mice," "The Golden Flowerpot," etc. 458pp. 5⅜ x 8½. 21793-0

FROM FETISH TO GOD IN ANCIENT EGYPT, E. A. Wallis Budge. Rich detailed survey of Egyptian conception of "God" and gods, magic, cult of animals, Osiris, more. Also, superb English translations of hymns and legends. 240 illustrations. 545pp. 5⅜ x 8½. 25803-3

FRENCH STORIES/CONTES FRANÇAIS: A Dual-Language Book, Wallace Fowlie. Ten stories by French masters, Voltaire to Camus: "Micromegas" by Voltaire; "The Atheist's Mass" by Balzac; "Minuet" by de Maupassant; "The Guest" by Camus, six more. Excellent English translations on facing pages. Also French-English vocabulary list, exercises, more. 352pp. 5⅜ x 8½. 26443-2

CHICAGO AT THE TURN OF THE CENTURY IN PHOTOGRAPHS: 122 Historic Views from the Collections of the Chicago Historical Society, Larry A. Viskochil. Rare large-format prints offer detailed views of City Hall, State Street, the Loop, Hull House, Union Station, many other landmarks, circa 1904-1913. Introduction. Captions. Maps. 144pp. 9⅜ x 12¼. 24656-6

OLD BROOKLYN IN EARLY PHOTOGRAPHS, 1865-1929, William Lee Younger. Luna Park, Gravesend race track, construction of Grand Army Plaza, moving of Hotel Brighton, etc. 157 previously unpublished photographs. 165pp. 8⅞ x 11¾. 23587-4

THE MYTHS OF THE NORTH AMERICAN INDIANS, Lewis Spence. Rich anthology of the myths and legends of the Algonquins, Iroquois, Pawnees and Sioux, prefaced by an extensive historical and ethnological commentary. 36 illustrations. 480pp. 5⅜ x 8½. 25967-6

AN ENCYCLOPEDIA OF BATTLES: Accounts of Over 1,560 Battles from 1479 B.C. to the Present, David Eggenberger. Essential details of every major battle in recorded history from the first battle of Megiddo in 1479 B.C. to Grenada in 1984. List of Battle Maps. New Appendix covering the years 1967-1984. Index. 99 illustrations. 544pp. 6½ x 9¼. 24913-1

SAILING ALONE AROUND THE WORLD, Captain Joshua Slocum. First man to sail around the world, alone, in small boat. One of great feats of seamanship told in delightful manner. 67 illustrations. 294pp. 5⅜ x 8½. 20326-3

ANARCHISM AND OTHER ESSAYS, Emma Goldman. Powerful, penetrating, prophetic essays on direct action, role of minorities, prison reform, puritan hypocrisy, violence, etc. 271pp. 5⅜ x 8½. 22484-8

MYTHS OF THE HINDUS AND BUDDHISTS, Ananda K. Coomaraswamy and Sister Nivedita. Great stories of the epics; deeds of Krishna, Shiva, taken from puranas, Vedas, folk tales; etc. 32 illustrations. 400pp. 5⅜ x 8½. 21759-0

THE TRAUMA OF BIRTH, Otto Rank. Rank's controversial thesis that anxiety neurosis is caused by profound psychological trauma which occurs at birth. 256pp. 5⅜ x 8½. 27974-X

A THEOLOGICO-POLITICAL TREATISE, Benedict Spinoza. Also contains unfinished Political Treatise. Great classic on religious liberty, theory of government on common consent. R. Elwes translation. Total of 421pp. 5⅜ x 8½. 20249-6

MY BONDAGE AND MY FREEDOM, Frederick Douglass. Born a slave, Douglass became outspoken force in antislavery movement. The best of Douglass' autobiographies. Graphic description of slave life. 464pp. 5⅜ x 8½. 22457-0

FOLLOWING THE EQUATOR: A Journey Around the World, Mark Twain. Fascinating humorous account of 1897 voyage to Hawaii, Australia, India, New Zealand, etc. Ironic, bemused reports on peoples, customs, climate, flora and fauna, politics, much more. 197 illustrations. 720pp. 5⅜ x 8½. 26113-1

THE PEOPLE CALLED SHAKERS, Edward D. Andrews. Definitive study of Shakers: origins, beliefs, practices, dances, social organization, furniture and crafts, etc. 33 illustrations. 351pp. 5⅜ x 8½. 21081-2

THE MYTHS OF GREECE AND ROME, H. A. Guerber. A classic of mythology, generously illustrated, long prized for its simple, graphic, accurate retelling of the principal myths of Greece and Rome, and for its commentary on their origins and significance. With 64 illustrations by Michelangelo, Raphael, Titian, Rubens, Canova, Bernini and others. 480pp. 5⅜ x 8½. 27584-1

PSYCHOLOGY OF MUSIC, Carl E. Seashore. Classic work discusses music as a medium from psychological viewpoint. Clear treatment of physical acoustics, auditory apparatus, sound perception, development of musical skills, nature of musical feeling, host of other topics. 88 figures. 408pp. 5⅜ x 8½. 21851-1

THE PHILOSOPHY OF HISTORY, Georg W. Hegel. Great classic of Western thought develops concept that history is not chance but rational process, the evolution of freedom. 457pp. 5⅜ x 8½. 20112-0

THE BOOK OF TEA, Kakuzo Okakura. Minor classic of the Orient: entertaining, charming explanation, interpretation of traditional Japanese culture in terms of tea ceremony. 94pp. 5⅜ x 8½. 20070-1

LIFE IN ANCIENT EGYPT, Adolf Erman. Fullest, most thorough, detailed older account with much not in more recent books, domestic life, religion, magic, medicine, commerce, much more. Many illustrations reproduce tomb paintings, carvings, hieroglyphs, etc. 597pp. 5⅜ x 8½. 22632-8

SUNDIALS, Their Theory and Construction, Albert Waugh. Far and away the best, most thorough coverage of ideas, mathematics concerned, types, construction, adjusting anywhere. Simple, nontechnical treatment allows even children to build several of these dials. Over 100 illustrations. 230pp. 5⅜ x 8½. 22947-5

THEORETICAL HYDRODYNAMICS, L. M. Milne-Thomson. Classic exposition of the mathematical theory of fluid motion, applicable to both hydrodynamics and aerodynamics. Over 600 exercises. 768pp. 6⅛ x 9¼. 68970-0

SONGS OF EXPERIENCE: Facsimile Reproduction with 26 Plates in Full Color, William Blake. 26 full-color plates from a rare 1826 edition. Includes "The Tyger," "London," "Holy Thursday," and other poems. Printed text of poems. 48pp. 5¼ x 7. 24636-1

OLD-TIME VIGNETTES IN FULL COLOR, Carol Belanger Grafton (ed.). Over 390 charming, often sentimental illustrations, selected from archives of Victorian graphics—pretty women posing, children playing, food, flowers, kittens and puppies, smiling cherubs, birds and butterflies, much more. All copyright-free. 48pp. 9¼ x 12¼. 27269-9

PERSPECTIVE FOR ARTISTS, Rex Vicat Cole. Depth, perspective of sky and sea, shadows, much more, not usually covered. 391 diagrams, 81 reproductions of drawings and paintings. 279pp. 5⅜ x 8½. 22487-2

DRAWING THE LIVING FIGURE, Joseph Sheppard. Innovative approach to artistic anatomy focuses on specifics of surface anatomy, rather than muscles and bones. Over 170 drawings of live models in front, back and side views, and in widely varying poses. Accompanying diagrams. 177 illustrations. Introduction. Index. 144pp. 8⅜ x11¼. 26723-7

GOTHIC AND OLD ENGLISH ALPHABETS: 100 Complete Fonts, Dan X. Solo. Add power, elegance to posters, signs, other graphics with 100 stunning copyright-free alphabets: Blackstone, Dolbey, Germania, 97 more–including many lower-case, numerals, punctuation marks. 104pp. 8⅛ x 11. 24695-7

HOW TO DO BEADWORK, Mary White. Fundamental book on craft from simple projects to five-bead chains and woven works. 106 illustrations. 142pp. 5⅜ x 8. 20697-1

THE BOOK OF WOOD CARVING, Charles Marshall Sayers. Finest book for beginners discusses fundamentals and offers 34 designs. "Absolutely first rate . . . well thought out and well executed."–E. J. Tangerman. 118pp. 7¾ x 10⅝. 23654-4

ILLUSTRATED CATALOG OF CIVIL WAR MILITARY GOODS: Union Army Weapons, Insignia, Uniform Accessories, and Other Equipment, Schuyler, Hartley, and Graham. Rare, profusely illustrated 1846 catalog includes Union Army uniform and dress regulations, arms and ammunition, coats, insignia, flags, swords, rifles, etc. 226 illustrations. 160pp. 9 x 12. 24939-5

WOMEN'S FASHIONS OF THE EARLY 1900s: An Unabridged Republication of "New York Fashions, 1909," National Cloak & Suit Co. Rare catalog of mail-order fashions documents women's and children's clothing styles shortly after the turn of the century. Captions offer full descriptions, prices. Invaluable resource for fashion, costume historians. Approximately 725 illustrations. 128pp. 8⅜ x 11¼. 27276-1

THE 1912 AND 1915 GUSTAV STICKLEY FURNITURE CATALOGS, Gustav Stickley. With over 200 detailed illustrations and descriptions, these two catalogs are essential reading and reference materials and identification guides for Stickley furniture. Captions cite materials, dimensions and prices. 112pp. 6½ x 9¼. 26676-1

EARLY AMERICAN LOCOMOTIVES, John H. White, Jr. Finest locomotive engravings from early 19th century: historical (1804–74), main-line (after 1870), special, foreign, etc. 147 plates. 142pp. 11⅜ x 8¼. 22772-3

THE TALL SHIPS OF TODAY IN PHOTOGRAPHS, Frank O. Braynard. Lavishly illustrated tribute to nearly 100 majestic contemporary sailing vessels: Amerigo Vespucci, Clearwater, Constitution, Eagle, Mayflower, Sea Cloud, Victory, many more. Authoritative captions provide statistics, background on each ship. 190 black-and-white photographs and illustrations. Introduction. 128pp. 8⅞ x 11¾. 27163-3

CATALOG OF DOVER BOOKS

LITTLE BOOK OF EARLY AMERICAN CRAFTS AND TRADES, Peter Stockham (ed.). 1807 children's book explains crafts and trades: baker, hatter, cooper, potter, and many others. 23 copperplate illustrations. 140pp. 4⅝ x 6.   23336-7

VICTORIAN FASHIONS AND COSTUMES FROM HARPER'S BAZAR, 1867–1898, Stella Blum (ed.). Day costumes, evening wear, sports clothes, shoes, hats, other accessories in over 1,000 detailed engravings. 320pp. 9⅜ x 12¼. 22990-4

GUSTAV STICKLEY, THE CRAFTSMAN, Mary Ann Smith. Superb study surveys broad scope of Stickley's achievement, especially in architecture. Design philosophy, rise and fall of the Craftsman empire, descriptions and floor plans for many Craftsman houses, more. 86 black-and-white halftones. 31 line illustrations. Introduction 208pp. 6½ x 9¼.   27210-9

THE LONG ISLAND RAIL ROAD IN EARLY PHOTOGRAPHS, Ron Ziel. Over 220 rare photos, informative text document origin (1844) and development of rail service on Long Island. Vintage views of early trains, locomotives, stations, passengers, crews, much more. Captions. 8⅞ x 11¾.   26301-0

VOYAGE OF THE LIBERDADE, Joshua Slocum. Great 19th-century mariner's thrilling, first-hand account of the wreck of his ship off South America, the 35-foot boat he built from the wreckage, and its remarkable voyage home. 128pp. 5⅜ x 8½.
40022-0

TEN BOOKS ON ARCHITECTURE, Vitruvius. The most important book ever written on architecture. Early Roman aesthetics, technology, classical orders, site selection, all other aspects. Morgan translation. 331pp. 5⅜ x 8½.   20645-9

THE HUMAN FIGURE IN MOTION, Eadweard Muybridge. More than 4,500 stopped-action photos, in action series, showing undraped men, women, children jumping, lying down, throwing, sitting, wrestling, carrying, etc. 390pp. 7⅞ x 10⅝.
20204-6 Clothbd.

TREES OF THE EASTERN AND CENTRAL UNITED STATES AND CANADA, William M. Harlow. Best one-volume guide to 140 trees. Full descriptions, woodlore, range, etc. Over 600 illustrations. Handy size. 288pp. 4½ x 6⅜.   20395-6

SONGS OF WESTERN BIRDS, Dr. Donald J. Borror. Complete song and call repertoire of 60 western species, including flycatchers, juncoes, cactus wrens, many more–includes fully illustrated booklet.   Cassette and manual 99913-0

GROWING AND USING HERBS AND SPICES, Milo Miloradovich. Versatile handbook provides all the information needed for cultivation and use of all the herbs and spices available in North America. 4 illustrations. Index. Glossary. 236pp. 5⅜ x 8½.
25058-X

BIG BOOK OF MAZES AND LABYRINTHS, Walter Shepherd. 50 mazes and labyrinths in all–classical, solid, ripple, and more–in one great volume. Perfect inexpensive puzzler for clever youngsters. Full solutions. 112pp. 8⅛ x 11.   22951-3

CATALOG OF DOVER BOOKS

PIANO TUNING, J. Cree Fischer. Clearest, best book for beginner, amateur. Simple repairs, raising dropped notes, tuning by easy method of flattened fifths. No previous skills needed. 4 illustrations. 201pp. 5⅜ x 8½.   23267-0

HINTS TO SINGERS, Lillian Nordica. Selecting the right teacher, developing confidence, overcoming stage fright, and many other important skills receive thoughtful discussion in this indispensible guide, written by a world-famous diva of four decades' experience. 96pp. 5⅜ x 8½.   40094-8

THE COMPLETE NONSENSE OF EDWARD LEAR, Edward Lear. All nonsense limericks, zany alphabets, Owl and Pussycat, songs, nonsense botany, etc., illustrated by Lear. Total of 320pp. 5⅜ x 8½. (Available in U.S. only.)   20167-8

VICTORIAN PARLOUR POETRY: An Annotated Anthology, Michael R. Turner. 117 gems by Longfellow, Tennyson, Browning, many lesser-known poets. "The Village Blacksmith," "Curfew Must Not Ring Tonight," "Only a Baby Small," dozens more, often difficult to find elsewhere. Index of poets, titles, first lines. xxiii + 325pp. 5⅜ x 8¼.   27044-0

DUBLINERS, James Joyce. Fifteen stories offer vivid, tightly focused observations of the lives of Dublin's poorer classes. At least one, "The Dead," is considered a masterpiece. Reprinted complete and unabridged from standard edition. 160pp. 5³⁄₁₆ x 8¼.   26870-5

GREAT WEIRD TALES: 14 Stories by Lovecraft, Blackwood, Machen and Others, S. T. Joshi (ed.). 14 spellbinding tales, including "The Sin Eater," by Fiona McLeod, "The Eye Above the Mantel," by Frank Belknap Long, as well as renowned works by R. H. Barlow, Lord Dunsany, Arthur Machen, W. C. Morrow and eight other masters of the genre. 256pp. 5⅜ x 8½. (Available in U.S. only.)   40436-6

THE BOOK OF THE SACRED MAGIC OF ABRAMELIN THE MAGE, translated by S. MacGregor Mathers. Medieval manuscript of ceremonial magic. Basic document in Aleister Crowley, Golden Dawn groups. 268pp. 5⅜ x 8½.   23211-5

NEW RUSSIAN-ENGLISH AND ENGLISH-RUSSIAN DICTIONARY, M. A. O'Brien. This is a remarkably handy Russian dictionary, containing a surprising amount of information, including over 70,000 entries. 366pp. 4½ x 6⅛.   20208-9

HISTORIC HOMES OF THE AMERICAN PRESIDENTS, Second, Revised Edition, Irvin Haas. A traveler's guide to American Presidential homes, most open to the public, depicting and describing homes occupied by every American President from George Washington to George Bush. With visiting hours, admission charges, travel routes. 175 photographs. Index. 160pp. 8¼ x 11.   26751-2

NEW YORK IN THE FORTIES, Andreas Feininger. 162 brilliant photographs by the well-known photographer, formerly with *Life* magazine. Commuters, shoppers, Times Square at night, much else from city at its peak. Captions by John von Hartz. 181pp. 9¼ x 10¾.   23585-8

INDIAN SIGN LANGUAGE, William Tomkins. Over 525 signs developed by Sioux and other tribes. Written instructions and diagrams. Also 290 pictographs. 111pp. 6⅛ x 9¼.   22029-X

CATALOG OF DOVER BOOKS

ANATOMY: A Complete Guide for Artists, Joseph Sheppard. A master of figure drawing shows artists how to render human anatomy convincingly. Over 460 illustrations. 224pp. 8⅜ x 11¼. 27279-6

MEDIEVAL CALLIGRAPHY: Its History and Technique, Marc Drogin. Spirited history, comprehensive instruction manual covers 13 styles (ca. 4th century through 15th). Excellent photographs; directions for duplicating medieval techniques with modern tools. 224pp. 8⅜ x 11¼. 26142-5

DRIED FLOWERS: How to Prepare Them, Sarah Whitlock and Martha Rankin. Complete instructions on how to use silica gel, meal and borax, perlite aggregate, sand and borax, glycerine and water to create attractive permanent flower arrangements. 12 illustrations. 32pp. 5⅜ x 8½. 21802-3

EASY-TO-MAKE BIRD FEEDERS FOR WOODWORKERS, Scott D. Campbell. Detailed, simple-to-use guide for designing, constructing, caring for and using feeders. Text, illustrations for 12 classic and contemporary designs. 96pp. 5⅜ x 8½. 25847-5

SCOTTISH WONDER TALES FROM MYTH AND LEGEND, Donald A. Mackenzie. 16 lively tales tell of giants rumbling down mountainsides, of a magic wand that turns stone pillars into warriors, of gods and goddesses, evil hags, powerful forces and more. 240pp. 5⅜ x 8½. 29677-6

THE HISTORY OF UNDERCLOTHES, C. Willett Cunnington and Phyllis Cunnington. Fascinating, well-documented survey covering six centuries of English undergarments, enhanced with over 100 illustrations: 12th-century laced-up bodice, footed long drawers (1795), 19th-century bustles, 19th-century corsets for men, Victorian "bust improvers," much more. 272pp. 5⅜ x 8¼. 27124-2

ARTS AND CRAFTS FURNITURE: The Complete Brooks Catalog of 1912, Brooks Manufacturing Co. Photos and detailed descriptions of more than 150 now very collectible furniture designs from the Arts and Crafts movement depict davenports, settees, buffets, desks, tables, chairs, bedsteads, dressers and more, all built of solid, quarter-sawed oak. Invaluable for students and enthusiasts of antiques, Americana and the decorative arts. 80pp. 6½ x 9¼. 27471-3

WILBUR AND ORVILLE: A Biography of the Wright Brothers, Fred Howard. Definitive, crisply written study tells the full story of the brothers' lives and work. A vividly written biography, unparalleled in scope and color, that also captures the spirit of an extraordinary era. 560pp. 6⅛ x 9¼. 40297-5

THE ARTS OF THE SAILOR: Knotting, Splicing and Ropework, Hervey Garrett Smith. Indispensable shipboard reference covers tools, basic knots and useful hitches; handsewing and canvas work, more. Over 100 illustrations. Delightful reading for sea lovers. 256pp. 5⅜ x 8½. 26440-8

FRANK LLOYD WRIGHT'S FALLINGWATER: The House and Its History, Second, Revised Edition, Donald Hoffmann. A total revision—both in text and illustrations—of the standard document on Fallingwater, the boldest, most personal architectural statement of Wright's mature years, updated with valuable new material from the recently opened Frank Lloyd Wright Archives. "Fascinating"–*The New York Times*. 116 illustrations. 128pp. 9¼ x 10¾. 27430-6

CATALOG OF DOVER BOOKS

PHOTOGRAPHIC SKETCHBOOK OF THE CIVIL WAR, Alexander Gardner. 100 photos taken on field during the Civil War. Famous shots of Manassas Harper's Ferry, Lincoln, Richmond, slave pens, etc. 244pp. 10⅝ x 8¼. 22731-6

FIVE ACRES AND INDEPENDENCE, Maurice G. Kains. Great back-to-the-land classic explains basics of self-sufficient farming. The one book to get. 95 illustrations. 397pp. 5⅜ x 8½. 20974-1

SONGS OF EASTERN BIRDS, Dr. Donald J. Borror. Songs and calls of 60 species most common to eastern U.S.: warblers, woodpeckers, flycatchers, thrushes, larks, many more in high-quality recording. Cassette and manual 99912-2

A MODERN HERBAL, Margaret Grieve. Much the fullest, most exact, most useful compilation of herbal material. Gigantic alphabetical encyclopedia, from aconite to zedoary, gives botanical information, medical properties, folklore, economic uses, much else. Indispensable to serious reader. 161 illustrations. 888pp. 6½ x 9¼. 2-vol. set. (Available in U.S. only.) Vol. I: 22798-7
Vol. II: 22799-5

HIDDEN TREASURE MAZE BOOK, Dave Phillips. Solve 34 challenging mazes accompanied by heroic tales of adventure. Evil dragons, people-eating plants, blood-thirsty giants, many more dangerous adversaries lurk at every twist and turn. 34 mazes, stories, solutions. 48pp. 8¼ x 11. 24566-7

LETTERS OF W. A. MOZART, Wolfgang A. Mozart. Remarkable letters show bawdy wit, humor, imagination, musical insights, contemporary musical world; includes some letters from Leopold Mozart. 276pp. 5⅜ x 8½. 22859-2

BASIC PRINCIPLES OF CLASSICAL BALLET, Agrippina Vaganova. Great Russian theoretician, teacher explains methods for teaching classical ballet. 118 illustrations. 175pp. 5⅜ x 8½. 22036-2

THE JUMPING FROG, Mark Twain. Revenge edition. The original story of The Celebrated Jumping Frog of Calaveras County, a hapless French translation, and Twain's hilarious "retranslation" from the French. 12 illustrations. 66pp. 5⅜ x 8½. 22686-7

BEST REMEMBERED POEMS, Martin Gardner (ed.). The 126 poems in this superb collection of 19th- and 20th-century British and American verse range from Shelley's "To a Skylark" to the impassioned "Renascence" of Edna St. Vincent Millay and to Edward Lear's whimsical "The Owl and the Pussycat." 224pp. 5⅜ x 8½. 27165-X

COMPLETE SONNETS, William Shakespeare. Over 150 exquisite poems deal with love, friendship, the tyranny of time, beauty's evanescence, death and other themes in language of remarkable power, precision and beauty. Glossary of archaic terms. 80pp. 5³⁄₁₆ x 8¼. 26686-9

THE BATTLES THAT CHANGED HISTORY, Fletcher Pratt. Eminent historian profiles 16 crucial conflicts, ancient to modern, that changed the course of civilization. 352pp. 5⅜ x 8½. 41129-X

CATALOG OF DOVER BOOKS

THE WIT AND HUMOR OF OSCAR WILDE, Alvin Redman (ed.). More than 1,000 ripostes, paradoxes, wisecracks: Work is the curse of the drinking classes; I can resist everything except temptation; etc. 258pp. 5⅜ x 8½. 20602-5

SHAKESPEARE LEXICON AND QUOTATION DICTIONARY, Alexander Schmidt. Full definitions, locations, shades of meaning in every word in plays and poems. More than 50,000 exact quotations. 1,485pp. 6½ x 9¼. 2-vol. set.
Vol. 1: 22726-X
Vol. 2: 22727-8

SELECTED POEMS, Emily Dickinson. Over 100 best-known, best-loved poems by one of America's foremost poets, reprinted from authoritative early editions. No comparable edition at this price. Index of first lines. 64pp. 5³⁄₁₆ x 8¼. 26466-1

THE INSIDIOUS DR. FU-MANCHU, Sax Rohmer. The first of the popular mystery series introduces a pair of English detectives to their archnemesis, the diabolical Dr. Fu-Manchu. Flavorful atmosphere, fast-paced action, and colorful characters enliven this classic of the genre. 208pp. 5³⁄₁₆ x 8¼. 29898-1

THE MALLEUS MALEFICARUM OF KRAMER AND SPRENGER, translated by Montague Summers. Full text of most important witchhunter's "bible," used by both Catholics and Protestants. 278pp. 6⅝ x 10. 22802-9

SPANISH STORIES/CUENTOS ESPAÑOLES: A Dual-Language Book, Angel Flores (ed.). Unique format offers 13 great stories in Spanish by Cervantes, Borges, others. Faithful English translations on facing pages. 352pp. 5⅜ x 8½. 25399-6

GARDEN CITY, LONG ISLAND, IN EARLY PHOTOGRAPHS, 1869–1919, Mildred H. Smith. Handsome treasury of 118 vintage pictures, accompanied by carefully researched captions, document the Garden City Hotel fire (1899), the Vanderbilt Cup Race (1908), the first airmail flight departing from the Nassau Boulevard Aerodrome (1911), and much more. 96pp. 8⅞ x 11¾. 40669-5

OLD QUEENS, N.Y., IN EARLY PHOTOGRAPHS, Vincent F. Seyfried and William Asadorian. Over 160 rare photographs of Maspeth, Jamaica, Jackson Heights, and other areas. Vintage views of DeWitt Clinton mansion, 1939 World's Fair and more. Captions. 192pp. 8⅞ x 11. 26358-4

CAPTURED BY THE INDIANS: 15 Firsthand Accounts, 1750-1870, Frederick Drimmer. Astounding true historical accounts of grisly torture, bloody conflicts, relentless pursuits, miraculous escapes and more, by people who lived to tell the tale. 384pp. 5⅜ x 8½. 24901-8

THE WORLD'S GREAT SPEECHES (Fourth Enlarged Edition), Lewis Copeland, Lawrence W. Lamm, and Stephen J. McKenna. Nearly 300 speeches provide public speakers with a wealth of updated quotes and inspiration–from Pericles' funeral oration and William Jennings Bryan's "Cross of Gold Speech" to Malcolm X's powerful words on the Black Revolution and Earl of Spenser's tribute to his sister, Diana, Princess of Wales. 944pp. 5⅜ x 8⅜. 40903-1

THE BOOK OF THE SWORD, Sir Richard F. Burton. Great Victorian scholar/adventurer's eloquent, erudite history of the "queen of weapons"–from prehistory to early Roman Empire. Evolution and development of early swords, variations (sabre, broadsword, cutlass, scimitar, etc.), much more. 336pp. 6⅛ x 9¼. 25434-8

AUTOBIOGRAPHY: The Story of My Experiments with Truth, Mohandas K. Gandhi. Boyhood, legal studies, purification, the growth of the Satyagraha (nonviolent protest) movement. Critical, inspiring work of the man responsible for the freedom of India. 480pp. 5⅜ x 8½. (Available in U.S. only.) 24593-4

CELTIC MYTHS AND LEGENDS, T. W. Rolleston. Masterful retelling of Irish and Welsh stories and tales. Cuchulain, King Arthur, Deirdre, the Grail, many more. First paperback edition. 58 full-page illustrations. 512pp. 5⅜ x 8½. 26507-2

THE PRINCIPLES OF PSYCHOLOGY, William James. Famous long course complete, unabridged. Stream of thought, time perception, memory, experimental methods; great work decades ahead of its time. 94 figures. 1,391pp. 5⅜ x 8½. 2-vol. set. Vol. I: 20381-6 Vol. II: 20382-4

THE WORLD AS WILL AND REPRESENTATION, Arthur Schopenhauer. Definitive English translation of Schopenhauer's life work, correcting more than 1,000 errors, omissions in earlier translations. Translated by E. F. J. Payne. Total of 1,269pp. 5⅜ x 8½. 2-vol. set. Vol. 1: 21761-2 Vol. 2: 21762-0

MAGIC AND MYSTERY IN TIBET, Madame Alexandra David-Neel. Experiences among lamas, magicians, sages, sorcerers, Bonpa wizards. A true psychic discovery. 32 illustrations. 321pp. 5⅜ x 8½. (Available in U.S. only.) 22682-4

THE EGYPTIAN BOOK OF THE DEAD, E. A. Wallis Budge. Complete reproduction of Ani's papyrus, finest ever found. Full hieroglyphic text, interlinear transliteration, word-for-word translation, smooth translation. 533pp. 6½ x 9¼. 21866-X

MATHEMATICS FOR THE NONMATHEMATICIAN, Morris Kline. Detailed, college-level treatment of mathematics in cultural and historical context, with numerous exercises. Recommended Reading Lists. Tables. Numerous figures. 641pp. 5⅜ x 8½. 24823-2

PROBABILISTIC METHODS IN THE THEORY OF STRUCTURES, Isaac Elishakoff. Well-written introduction covers the elements of the theory of probability from two or more random variables, the reliability of such multivariable structures, the theory of random function, Monte Carlo methods of treating problems incapable of exact solution, and more. Examples. 502pp. 5⅜ x 8½. 40691-1

THE RIME OF THE ANCIENT MARINER, Gustave Doré, S. T. Coleridge. Doré's finest work; 34 plates capture moods, subtleties of poem. Flawless full-size reproductions printed on facing pages with authoritative text of poem. "Beautiful. Simply beautiful."–*Publisher's Weekly.* 77pp. 9¼ x 12. 22305-1

NORTH AMERICAN INDIAN DESIGNS FOR ARTISTS AND CRAFTSPEOPLE, Eva Wilson. Over 360 authentic copyright-free designs adapted from Navajo blankets, Hopi pottery, Sioux buffalo hides, more. Geometrics, symbolic figures, plant and animal motifs, etc. 128pp. 8⅜ x 11. (Not for sale in the United Kingdom.) 25341-4

SCULPTURE: Principles and Practice, Louis Slobodkin. Step-by-step approach to clay, plaster, metals, stone; classical and modern. 253 drawings, photos. 255pp. 8⅛ x 11. 22960-2

THE INFLUENCE OF SEA POWER UPON HISTORY, 1660–1783, A. T. Mahan. Influential classic of naval history and tactics still used as text in war colleges. First paperback edition. 4 maps. 24 battle plans. 640pp. 5⅜ x 8½. 25509-3

CATALOG OF DOVER BOOKS

THE STORY OF THE TITANIC AS TOLD BY ITS SURVIVORS, Jack Winocour (ed.). What it was really like. Panic, despair, shocking inefficiency, and a little heroism. More thrilling than any fictional account. 26 illustrations. 320pp. 5⅜ x 8½. 20610-6

FAIRY AND FOLK TALES OF THE IRISH PEASANTRY, William Butler Yeats (ed.). Treasury of 64 tales from the twilight world of Celtic myth and legend: "The Soul Cages," "The Kildare Pooka," "King O'Toole and his Goose," many more. Introduction and Notes by W. B. Yeats. 352pp. 5⅜ x 8½. 26941-8

BUDDHIST MAHAYANA TEXTS, E. B. Cowell and others (eds.). Superb, accurate translations of basic documents in Mahayana Buddhism, highly important in history of religions. The Buddha-karita of Asvaghosha, Larger Sukhavativyuha, more. 448pp. 5⅜ x 8½. 25552-2

ONE TWO THREE . . . INFINITY: Facts and Speculations of Science, George Gamow. Great physicist's fascinating, readable overview of contemporary science: number theory, relativity, fourth dimension, entropy, genes, atomic structure, much more. 128 illustrations. Index. 352pp. 5⅜ x 8½. 25664-2

EXPERIMENTATION AND MEASUREMENT, W. J. Youden. Introductory manual explains laws of measurement in simple terms and offers tips for achieving accuracy and minimizing errors. Mathematics of measurement, use of instruments, experimenting with machines. 1994 edition. Foreword. Preface. Introduction. Epilogue. Selected Readings. Glossary. Index. Tables and figures. 128pp. 5⅜ x 8½. 40451-X

DALÍ ON MODERN ART: The Cuckolds of Antiquated Modern Art, Salvador Dalí. Influential painter skewers modern art and its practitioners. Outrageous evaluations of Picasso, Cézanne, Turner, more. 15 renderings of paintings discussed. 44 calligraphic decorations by Dalí. 96pp. 5⅜ x 8½. (Available in U.S. only.) 29220-7

ANTIQUE PLAYING CARDS: A Pictorial History, Henry René D'Allemagne. Over 900 elaborate, decorative images from rare playing cards (14th–20th centuries): Bacchus, death, dancing dogs, hunting scenes, royal coats of arms, players cheating, much more. 96pp. 9¼ x 12¼. 29265-7

MAKING FURNITURE MASTERPIECES: 30 Projects with Measured Drawings, Franklin H. Gottshall. Step-by-step instructions, illustrations for constructing handsome, useful pieces, among them a Sheraton desk, Chippendale chair, Spanish desk, Queen Anne table and a William and Mary dressing mirror. 224pp. 8⅛ x 11¼. 29338-6

THE FOSSIL BOOK: A Record of Prehistoric Life, Patricia V. Rich et al. Profusely illustrated definitive guide covers everything from single-celled organisms and dinosaurs to birds and mammals and the interplay between climate and man. Over 1,500 illustrations. 760pp. 7½ x 10⅛. 29371-8